Killed in a traffic collision, the last thing Lana expected was to wake up under the gaze of two very confused aliens. They were expecting a tribute for the upcoming challenges and instead they got her. Refusing to be one female down, they stick Lana into the line-up, but when the challenges are over and the Warriors choose their females, she's left unchosen. She understands why. All the other females have stars on their cheeks, emphasizing their blood purity. She's unmarked, and in this world, it means her blood is weak, useless.

Lana hopes she might be able to go home somehow — deceased status notwithstanding — seeing as no one wanted her, but Warrior Vall Ridian charges in late. He's not impressed to be left with a starless female, but as the Administrator running the challenges informs him, shit blood's better than no blood. It only takes one sip of Lana's blood for Vall to realize that she's not a starless female. In fact, her blood is the strongest he's ever tasted.

Lana is the key to unlocking the Warriors' most sacred — and most sorely lost — treasure. With her, they will be able to transform into fully fledged dragons. It's an incredible gift, but also a dangerous one, as Vall and the pack discover when Lana is stolen from them by a rival pack who have discovered who she is and what she can do. They'll have to fight to get her back and then to keep her safe.

Seven Stars
Copyright © 2020 Charli Mac
ISBN: 978-1-4874-3122-8
Cover art by Martine Jardin

Published by eXtasy Books Inc or
Devine Destinies, an imprint of eXtasy Books Inc

Look for us online at:
www.eXtasybooks.com or www.devinedestinies.com

Seven Stars
Trinia Chronicles Book 1

By

Charli Mac

DEDICATION

*For Clare, who trawled charity shops to find me my first smut
when we were poor university students.*

CHAPTER ONE

The weather was foul. My windscreen wipers were going top speed and they still couldn't keep up with the deluge turning the world outside into a blur. In the seat beside me, the engagement party cake I'd spent all morning decorating wobbled as I took a corner too fast.

"Don't you dare," I muttered, reaching out a hand and snagging the box.

I was late, which I hated, but the actual party didn't start until 7.30 p.m. and according to the satnav I'd be there at 6.43 p.m. — scrap that, 6.42 p.m. — so I should be in and out before any guests turned up.

There wasn't much traffic on the freeway and I lucked out with traffic lights, so it was only 6.36 p.m. when I steered my battered Ford Focus into the car park of the upmarket hotel my clients had chosen to celebrate their forthcoming union. Parking in the Pickup zone and ignoring the sign that warned caterers and tradespeople against doing exactly what I was about to do, I tugged on my slicker and pulled the hood up to cover my hair. When I killed the engine and yanked out the key, the sound of the rain was loud on the roof, drowning out the radio, which had a fault and wouldn't switch off unless I manually hit the power button.

Sliding out, I was soaked before I'd even rounded the car and carefully picked up my precious cargo. Thankfully, there were only a few short steps up to the main entrance and then I was inside, the brightly lit foyer pumping out elevator music and seeming like an oasis of calm compared to the storm

1

outside.

"Hi," I said, smiling as I approached the immaculately presented receptionist, who looked at me like I was the drowned cat I was sure I resembled. "I've got a cake for the Findlay-Robinson engagement party. Which function room are they in?"

The receptionist frowned and looked at the computer screen in front of her.

"We don't have any engagement parties today. Just a fiftieth birthday party and a bar mitzvah."

"I think you do," I replied, a little more shortly than the situation probably warranted. "Findlay-Robinson, April 17th, 7.30 p.m. start."

The woman, whose name tag identified her as Janice, looked back to her screen, fingers flying across the keyboard.

"'Fraid not," she said. "Have you got the date wrong?"

"Definitely not, the bride-to-be sent me a message just this morning."

A message in which she'd asked to change the color of the fondant and the wording of the iced message, which was why I was late.

"I'm sorry, I don't know what to say. Perhaps she gave you the wrong hotel? Could you call her and check?"

Giving an annoyed huff, I left the cake balanced precariously on the reception counter and stepped a few feet away to call. The phone rang for long enough that I thought no one was going to answer, but finally Angelica Findlay picked up.

"Hello?" she trilled.

"Angelica? Hi, it's Lana Murray. I'm at the hotel with your cake, but the receptionist here says there's no party under your name?"

There was a long pause and then Angelica gasped. "Oh my God! Are you at the Reynolds?"

"Well . . .yeah." My hand tightened on the handset as my

annoyance at the receptionist transferred rapidly to my client.

"I can't believe we forgot to tell you! We cancelled that! They wanted a ridiculous amount of money just for the function suite and it really wasn't worth it. We've moved the party to my mother-in-law's. It's over in Park Green."

"Park Green?" That was on the other side of town entirely.

"Yes." Another pause. "You will be able to make it on time, won't you? It's just, well, if you're late I really don't think we'll be able to pay you your full fee. We want the cake out on display as the guests come in, so they can see it. We'd never have spent so much on it otherwise."

Hauling in a deep breath through my nose, I checked my watch. 6.41 p.m.

"I'll try," I ground out.

"Excellent. I'll message you the address." A moment later I was listening to the dial tone. She'd hung up on me.

"If you're looking for someone to make your wedding cake, you can find some other mug," I hissed, stuffing the phone back into my jeans pocket.

"Did you get it all sorted?" the receptionist asked brightly when I returned to pick up my cake. The box was damp and slightly battered looking. Well, it was going to look a lot worse by the time it got to the party.

"Yes. Sorry." I aimed for a cheerful smile and failed miserably. "She changed the location and forgot to tell me."

"Oh dear." The look the receptionist gave me was sympathetic. "Work would be easy if only we didn't have to deal with the people, right?"

"Right." I managed a genuine smile this time before picking up the box and heading back out into the rain. It hadn't lessened any and now thunder was booming overhead.

The Ford Focus thought briefly about refusing to move, but I managed to coax it into starting and then took off double time, dashing out into traffic in front of a semi. My attention only half-focused on the thankfully quiet road, I pulled up the new address from Angelica's message and started to type it into the satnav.

"Come on, come on," I muttered, watching it load. *Route detected, time of arrival 7.27 p.m.* "Yes!"

Accelerating, I zoomed through a green light—right into the path of a truck, running the red.

I saw it out of the corner of my eye and had a second to turn, stare into huge headlights barreling right for me. There wasn't time for fear before it hit me, slamming into the side of the car and wrenching me sideways. My ears ringing, I stared in horror through the shattered windscreen, saw the road spinning as my little Focus aquaplaned across the surface. The cake took a nose-dive off the passenger seat, landing on its side on the floor, icing and sponge leeching out as the box disintegrated. My car careened off the road and down a steep embankment. An oak tree stopped its progress, metal crumpling around the thick trunk.

My head slammed into the steering wheel and the world finally went black.

CHAPTER TWO

"This is . . . not right." The strangely accented voice cut through oblivion.

My eyes fluttered open and then closed again as the bright lights drove painful spikes into my brain.

"Who is she? How did she get here?"

"Why are you asking me?"

"Do you see anyone else here to ask?"

"Well . . .there's always *her*."

The voices floated above me, preventing me from slipping back down into unconsciousness. Groaning, I flung an arm over my face. I felt hung over, but I hadn't been drinking after dropping off the cake at the damned Findlay-Robinson party, I —

I hadn't even made it to the party. A swift memory flashed in my mind — the car spinning out of control and then juddering down the embankment, slamming into a tree. Opening my eyes, I ignored the headache pounding at my temples and looked around. I expected to see an emergency room, doctors and gurneys, and all sorts of beeping machines.

Instead, I was lying on the floor of what looked more like a laboratory than a hospital, and the two men leaning over me and looking worried did not look like doctors. They were dressed wrongly, no scrubs or stethoscopes around their necks. More worryingly, I wasn't even sure they were men.

This was . . .not right.

One of them held a blanket in his hands. As I stared at him, he leaned forward and handed it to me. I clutched at it gratefully, abruptly aware that I was naked.

"Hello," he said, frowning. "Who are you? What are you doing here?"

What? I frowned back up at him. He was slender, with skin a dark shade of copper. His hair was braided tightly against his skull, a goatee neatly outlining a very pointed chin. He had no eyebrows and his ears were, well, they were pointed too.

The frowning one frowned even harder and looked at his companion. "She's not responding. Do you think she even understands us?" He didn't give his friend a moment to respond—or me a chance to correct him. "What are we supposed to do? The challenges start in a couple of hours, and all the rest of the offerings are already here. Where is the tribute from Farlin?"

The other one, who looked the same right down to his pointy little ears and, I noticed belatedly, slitted pupils, shrugged.

"I don't know, Rin. Maybe she is the tribute from Farlin?"

Rin snorted. "Does she look like she's from Farlin to you?"

"Well, no." Another shrug. "But I don't see anyone else coming through, do you?"

"All right." Rin took a deep breath and turned back to me. "Hello. Can you understand me?"

I nodded, wetting dry lips with my tongue. "I can understand you."

The nameless one brightened perceptibly, but Rin was still scowling.

"Who are you? You're not from Farlin, are you?"

"No. I . . .I don't know where that is." I looked around me again at the sterile, white room. There wasn't much in it except a couple of desks and a bed, plus some equipment on a bench behind it. Twisting round, though it hurt, my headache spiking, I saw the wall behind me was slightly different, its surface a shiny, wet looking metal, odd lights edging the outside. "Where am I?"

I scrambled, not wanting to be lying on the floor when panic was clawing at my insides and telling me something was very, very wrong.

Rin and his companion leaned forward and grabbed an arm each, helping me to my feet. Though they were both whippet-thin, they were strong, lifting me easily. They were tall, too, I noticed, my gaze level with the middle of their chests.

"You're in the receiving chamber," Rin told me. "We were expecting the tribute from Farlin, but you came through instead."

"Came . . .through?"

He gestured behind me with his chin and I turned to look once more at the glistening grey wall. "The transporter."

All right, then. Either I was in a coma — thank you, truck — or I'd died and old Pastor Jenkins had got the afterlife very wrong in his sermons.

"What are we going to do with her?" the second one repeated.

Rin rubbed at his goatee, looking at me thoughtfully. "We're a tribute down," he said. "But she's female. Not Triniun, not with those weird eyes, but look at her. She's probably compatible."

"What are you talking about?" I asked nervously. My gaze darted toward the exit, a set of double doors behind the two men, but I'd no idea what was out there and I was wearing nothing but a thin blanket.

"She hasn't got any stars," the nameless one objected.

Rin made a face. "Neither did the offerings from Unto and Killia. Someone will be grateful for them, nonetheless. Shit blood's better than no blood."

Blood? I took a step backward, my shoulders colliding with

the metal wall. I hissed, hunching forward, though the room was warm, the strange wall was icy cold.

"Put her in with the rest," Rin said decisively. "She's here now, she'll have to do."

I was taken to one of a dozen or so chambers that reminded me worryingly of prison cells. They were small cubes, maybe eight feet by eight feet, with three white walls and one final wall of glass where I could see the six cells opposite — and the "tributes" that inhabited them. They were all female and they all looked younger than my thirty-five years. They also all looked alien, with the pointed ears and skin tones that, while lighter than the males I'd seen, were definitely not human.

Though none of them looked particularly happy, they weren't screaming or pounding on the glass like I wanted to do. Most of them lounged on the narrow padded benches that were the only things in each cell, bar a small toilet and tiny sink.

A whirring noise made me pivot to stare at the back of my cell. A drawer opened out of the apparently seamless wall, and when I cautiously approached to investigate, I found a small pile of clothes. Relieved, I dropped the blanket and pulled on the sleeveless coral-colored tunic top and matching trousers, the same outfit the rest of the women were wearing. There was no underwear, but I definitely felt better being clothed. The drawer returned to the wall and nothing else looked set to appear — like, say, food — so I returned to the front of my cell. I saw the two women opposite had left their benches and were now pressed to the glass, looking over at me.

"You look strange," one of them said.

"And you don't have any stars," the other commented.

Stars. That was the second time I'd heard mention of that. And looking at the women opposite, it was obvious what they were referring to. Both had small stars tattooed beneath their left eyes, two stars on one woman, four on the other.

"No," I replied. "I don't. What are the stars about? What do they mean?"

The one with four stars raised an eyebrow. "They delineate the purity of your blood. So that the Warrior who claims you for his pack knows how much strength you will bring him."

"I see." I didn't, not really. "So, more stars is better?"

Four Stars snorted. "Of course. Five stars is almost entirely pure blood, not that that's been seen for a hundred years. Two is all right." She threw the woman in the neighboring cell a grimace. "But not to have any stars at all, well . . ." She lifted one shoulder in a delicate shrug. "Your Warriors would need to drain you dry just to stay strong enough to fight." The look she gave me was pitying. "Maybe your test was wrong."

"I haven't been tested," I said distractedly. The words *drain you dry* were spinning around my head, complete with visions of Bella Lugosi all dressed up as Dracula.

"You haven't? Why were you selected, then?" She gasped. "Are you a criminal? Did you volunteer to escape a death sentence?"

"No," I muttered, my attention down the corridor to where Rin was returning, this time accompanied by his friend and two others. They stopped in front of my cell.

"This is the one," Rin said, nodding at me. "We've scanned her and she seems compatible enough. I don't see that there's anything we can do except put her in. We can't be a tribute short."

"Please," I begged, fighting tears. "Tell me what's going on."

For the first time, Rin looked sympathetic. "We were expecting a tribute from Farlin to come through the gate," he told me, information I already knew. "Instead we got you."

"And?"

His strange, slitted gaze was steady on mine. "Warriors in need of new thralls have assembled. In a few moments, the challenges will begin. The Warriors will establish their dominance order and then . . ." He quirked his lips. "They'll choose their thralls."

CHAPTER THREE

Vall Ridian was pissed. The second sun was near to setting, which meant the thrall challenges were about to start, and he was still over a hundred leagues away trying to put down a group of sabers that just wouldn't die.

Snarling as one latched onto his back, elongated canines piercing skin and muscle, he reached back and grabbed at a fur covered arm and yanked. There was a snap as the beast's shoulder joint dislocated, but the bastard still didn't let go. It dug in deeper, head tossing as it worried at the wound it had inflicted. Vall roared, in anger more than pain, but his attempts to dislodge the saber were hampered by another coming at him head on, teeth snapping in front of his face.

"I have you!" The rough voice of his Second, Finn, came out of nowhere, flying in from the side and tearing the beast off his back. It hurt, the razor-sharp teeth causing even more damage as they were wrenched free, but at least Vall was released to concentrate on the saber in front of him. Getting a firm grip around its throat, he slashed at its ribs with his karambit, its curved blade finding the gap between the beast's ribs and cutting into a lung. It was a killing blow, but when he stepped back and released his grip on the saber's throat, he followed it up with a quick slice across the jugular to be certain. The creature dropped.

Breathing hard, sweat steaming from him in the cloying, humid air, he looked around. The clearing where they'd found the nest—just half a league from the village which had been stupid enough to sprout up on the edge of the forest—

11

was littered with bodies. The sabers wore only scraps of clothing, mostly bits and pieces they'd stolen either from the village or from the victims they snatched and then ate. They were a crude race, only just evolved from mindless animals, but they bred like nothing else. Trying to keep their numbers in check was pretty much all Vall and his pack did now.

The sabers fought with their own predatory gifts mostly, but they'd also started to use weapons made from wood and rocks, though there was the odd bit of metal here and there. Vall leaned down to look at one piece in particular, sliding it out from beneath the lax grasp of the hand that had died wielding it.

"What have you got there?" Finn asked, coming up on his shoulder.

"A knife," Vall murmured, turning it over in his hand.

It was a basic weapon, little more than a sharpened point wedged into a bit of horn, a leather wrap soaked in resin holding the whole thing together. Nothing this crude could be purchased in his world, which meant . . ."I think they made this."

"Metal work?" Finn raised his eyebrows, surprised, then shrugged. "You're bleeding," he commented. "It's pretty bad. You'll need stitches, I think."

"No time," Vall replied, tucking the find into his pocket. "We need to get out of here." He raised his voice. "Lyne, Jay, we're leaving."

The darkening sky was a claw tearing at Vall's insides. His dragon might be crippled and unable to erupt, but it was still there, still alive inside him, and it was painfully aware that the time to claim a thrall was slipping away. If they missed this offering, the pack would have to exist on synth blood for another year. Not such a big deal for Lyne or Jay, or even Finn, but Vall's dragon was too strong to survive on that muck. A year of it might well kill him, literally.

"Lyne! Jay!" Annoyed they hadn't responded immediately to his call—who was the fucking Alpha here?—he edged his voice with acid. Still they didn't turn, staring at something in the dark beyond the trees.

"Vall, you need to look at this," Jay shouted, looking back and waving him over.

His shoulder burning and his dragon agitated at the delay, Vall strode across the clearing, taking care to avoid stepping on the carpet of blood-splattered limbs. They didn't have time to do anything about the bodies, but that didn't mean he'd disrespect them by stomping all over them. Besides, the villages would probably want the meat. Though they were horrified the sabers would consume the victims they snatched, it was apparently perfectly all right for them to do the reverse, and they wouldn't appreciate boot-shaped bruises all over their next meal.

"What is it?" he growled, reaching the tree line.

Jay and Lyne didn't have to explain—he could see what it was as soon as Lyne pulled back a branch thick with foliage.

"Shit."

There, crouched among the thick grasses, was another saber. A female one. She had stripes running down the side of her face, emphasizing huge dark eyes that were looking at him with fear. At her feet, mewling and crawling all over each other, completely oblivious to the danger they were in, was a litter of tiny pups no more than a couple of days old.

"What are we going to do with them?" Jay asked.

The female turned watchful eyes on Jay. At his words, she crouched lower, hunkering protectively over her babies. Her mouth was open to show her teeth and she hissed, but she knew as well as they did that she was no match for the four of them.

"The villagers would want us to kill them," Lyne said quietly.

They would, because they might be tiny and harmless now, but the saber kits would grow, and then they'd just be more pests, deadly ones this time. But fuck if Vall could bring himself to pull a weapon on them or their mother. And if he couldn't do it, he wouldn't ask one of his pack to either.

"Can you understand me?" he asked. They had some words, he knew. It took a moment, but the female gave a small nod. "You need to leave. Go deeper into the forest, well away from the village." He paused. "If you don't, I'll have to come back and kill you. Understand?"

She was hesitant, and Vall felt impatience twist inside him. He did not have time for this.

"You need to go," he repeated.

"Ssstarving." The word came out mangled through a mouth not meant for speech, but Vall caught it.

"Then you'll have to hunt," he replied, unmoved. "That's your choice—go and live, or stay and die."

She glowered at him a moment longer, frustrated, but then she retracted her claws and started picking up her babies, one at a time.

"That way," Vall repeated, pointing deeper into the forest. "And don't come back. You hear me?"

The only response he got this time was a hiss as the female saber turned her back on him and started limping into the trees. Her back leg was mangled, he noticed, the skin healed over but the damage to the bones clearly permanent. No wonder she couldn't hunt. She'd have to find a way, though. The villagers wouldn't give a shit that she was lame, or that she had a tiny, innocent armful of cubs. They'd kill her, or haul Vall and his pack back here to do the job for them.

"You sure that was wise?" Finn asked, coming up behind them and watching the female disappear.

"You want to kill it?" Vall asked. Finn's silence was as good as a no. "Come on, we really need to move."

They might already be too late. The desperate worry pushed him into a run as he led his pack back to the village. Thank the gods the isolated community had invested in a transporter, or they would never have made it in time. Synth blood aside, Vall had a feeling he needed to be at this offering, and he had learned a long time ago never to ignore his instincts.

Chapter Four

We were going to be lucky enough to get to watch these challenges, apparently. The glass walls lifted up into the ceiling and we were all marched down the corridor into a space roughly the size and shape of a school auditorium. Four Stars walked in front of me, her steps light and her hair, a lighter tone than mine but thicker, almost like horsehair, twitching in its ponytail with barely contained excitement.

Not everyone felt the same. The woman behind me was sniffling. A quick glance back told me that she didn't have any stars. She also had a sickly, faded look about her. There were odd green splotches on her throat and jaw that I thought might be bruises. Looked like I wasn't the only one who didn't want to be here.

There weren't any benches or chairs for us to sit on, but there was a row of tiny platforms raised a step up from the slightly padded floor. We were walked along this row by Rin and three other males, each of us ushered to step up on one. I found myself somewhere in the middle of the line, between Four Stars and the unhealthy starless woman, who was crying in earnest now. I was trying to think of something comforting to say to her when doors burst open across from us and the group of warriors burst in.

Warriors was the word. These guys were not stringy-limbed like the unhelpful Rin, who'd ignored all the arguments and pleas I'd thrown at him, walking away after pronouncing me a compatible tribute and fit to take part in this science-fiction B-movie nightmare. They were walking

16

testosterone, thick with muscle and bristling with aggression. The first thing they did was walk the line of tributes, which allowed me to get a better look at them. Most had braided hair, though one or two had shaved theirs, drawing attention to the sharp points tipping their ears. They had masculine features, with hard jaws and pronounced cheekbones, and they all had darker skin tones, some copper-colored like Rin but others shimmering a silvery-grey or dark green in the overhead lights. And I could see a lot of skin, because though most were wearing full length trousers, they all had bare chests, biceps strapped with leather cuffs, the odd one wearing an additional strap diagonally across their pectorals.

Most of them passed right by me, glancing at my unmarked cheek and then dismissing me, but the woman beside me, the one with the four stars, got a lot of attention. The warriors postured and jostled for position, growling and flashing sharp teeth that made me think they definitely weren't a vegetarian race.

Rin appeared with a tablet in his hand, and the warriors reluctantly left the line of women, consulting briefly with Rin as he tapped away on the screen, conducting what I assumed was a roll call. Something had him frowning unhappily, but then he shrugged, uncaring, and tucked the tablet away.

That was as far as it went for administration. Alarmingly quickly after that, things descended into violence. Though I didn't understand how it was organized, they broke off into pairs and started fighting. They were short matches, though vicious and explosive, and I couldn't work out if they were aiming for first blood or just to get their opponent down on the mat. Each fight broke up differently and then the fighters would move on.

Things got more heated as the challenges progressed. Victories that at first had been celebrated with a pleased nod now received a triumphant roar, losses that had merited a shake of the head now came with a furious hiss or a fist pounding on the floor. Though I'd done nothing but stand and watch in horrified fascination, I was sweating and jittery with panic. It was obvious that things were drawing to a close.

After that, the warriors would come and pick a prize. With my unstarred cheek and my complete ignorance about where I was and what the world was like out there, I felt very much like the wooden spoon.

When the choosing started, it was all strangely civilized. The warriors, sweating and breathless, organized themselves into a line. Some looked smugly satisfied, others disappointed with their performance, but they were all eager.

It was no surprise even to me when the warrior at the front of the line went straight to the woman beside me with the four stars decorating her cheek. She watched him approach with breathless anticipation, a smile on her face. He went right up to her, not speaking a word and buried his nose in her neck. His muffled growl was echoed by a small groan from her, then she visibly flinched, hands coming up from her side to clutch at his shoulders. I couldn't tell if she was trying to hold him closer or push him away. Whichever it was, it lasted only a moment before her body went lax, head lolling back. She'd fainted. When the warrior pulled away, I saw why. Blood was smeared across his lips, and a lot more of it was seeping from a small wound on her throat, two lines dribbling down toward her collar bone.

Jesus Christ, they were actual blood drinkers.

I watched the rest of the choosing in a detached blur. My breathing was creeping toward hyperventilation and my body felt numb. I would have run, but even if I'd had anywhere to run to, I doubted my legs were up to the task. Right now they were struggling just to keep me upright.

We continued to stand there, women being picked off like we were choosing teams for hockey in PE, until eventually there were just the three of us left. Me, the crying woman beside me and one other who, when I craned my neck to see, also seemed to be unmarked. There were also, I couldn't help but notice, only two warriors left. Rin must have miscalculated, because it looked like I wasn't needed after all. Of course, the little shit wasn't around for me to explain that to him, and the warrior in front of me, narrow eyed as he prowled up and down taking in the three of us, didn't look in the mood to hear excuses.

I closed my eyes, wondering if praying would do any good since I didn't seem to be on Earth anymore and since I'd never actually believed in God. It couldn't hurt to try, though, so I started reciting what I could remember of the Lord's Prayer in my head while I waited to feel hot breath on my neck and clawed hands gripping my soft skin.

A squeal made me wrench my eyes open just in time to see the woman beside me hauled off her pedestal by the penultimate warrior. Her neck appeared unmolested, but he didn't look gentle as he flung her over one shoulder and stormed out. That left just the two of us. I looked over at the other woman, but she was staring fearfully at the remaining warrior—and rightly so, because he was stalking toward her, evidently having made up his mind while the warrior in front of him deliberated. Soon they were gone, too, and then it was just me, standing alone in the room.

Was that it?

Nobody had picked me, so what now?

I took a hesitant step forward, coming down off my platform and onto the slightly springy floor. No one appeared from either the double doors where the warriors had entered or the much more discreet side exit where Rin had disappeared to.

"Hello?" I called. "Is anybody there?"

No answer.

Nervous, but with my determination to leg it firming up with every moment that passed, I took one step, then another. My gaze flitted between the two exits, and I'd just made up my mind to head for the double doors—which I was pretty sure led to *out*—as fast as my wobbly legs could carry me, when Rin came through the side door. He was distracted, his gaze on his tablet, but before I had time to realize that and act on it, he looked up. His mouth pursed with unhappiness when he spotted me.

"You," he said.

"Me," I replied. I spread my hands helplessly. "No one picked me." I had never been so glad to be a reject. "Does that mean I can go home now?"

"Go home how?" he asked, sneering.

"Your . . .transporter thing."

"Where am I supposed to send you? I don't know where you're from."

"Earth," I told him, my pulse thudding with the sudden hope that my prayers might be answered and I might get out of this nightmare without so much as a probe story to tell.

"And where is Earth?" he asked scathingly. Just like that, my hopes came crashing down. I had no idea. The only thing I knew about space was that it was vast.

"I don't know," I admitted. I took a deep breath, trying to loosen the tightness in my chest. "What now, then?"

Rin didn't get a chance to answer. The double doors, the ones all the rest of the women had disappeared through, burst open for a second time, and another warrior stormed in. This one looked like he'd already been in the challenges, though I didn't recognize him. His braided hair was a mess and the leather strapping across his chest was torn. Was that blood I could see on his blue-tinted, slate grey skin? I thought it was.

"Fuck!" he shouted, coming to a halt and looking between me and Rin. "Am I too late?"

Rin recovered more quickly than I did, whipping out his tablet and consulting it briefly. "You are Vall Ridian?"

The warrior jerked his head in a nod, his face rolling over into one big scowl. "I am."

"You're right, you have missed the challenges. This is the only tribute left." Rin shrugged. "She's yours, if you want her."

If you want her? I wasn't sure whether to be outraged or terrified, though I quickly decided terrified was the better option as Vall's gaze narrowed on me and he stalked forward. He looked unimpressed, the ring piercing his upper lip glinting as he curled it.

"Unmarked?" he growled.

Rin gave another of those little shrugs that made me want to throttle him. "If you're late, you get what's left."

Gee, thanks.

Vall took another step closer, fixing the gaze of his silver eyes on me, their slitted pupils expanding and contracting as he looked me over. "She doesn't look like one of the starless," he commented thoughtfully. "She looks too healthy."

Rin shifted, looking suddenly cagey.

"Well . . ."

"I haven't been tested," I said, thinking it best to establish that before he took me away. I had no idea what might happen once he realized he'd been sold a dud, and I didn't want to find out. I was also holding on to the hope that he might just turn around and leave me there, give me the chance to get Rin to reconsider trying to send me home by just annoying him to death. "I'm not a tribute. I don't know how I got here, there was a . . .mix up."

A running-the-red-light-truck kind of mix up that I still hadn't quite wrapped my head around. There was still time for me to wake up, after all.

"You haven't been tested?" he asked, low voiced. His gaze

shifted to Rin, something feral and dangerous awakening within it, and Rin swallowed visibly.

"There wasn't time. We were a tribute down and the challenges were about to start. We did scan her, she's compatible."

Vall started toward me again, only this time his movements were slower, more sinuous. The silver in his eyes brightened as he reached for me, snagging one hand and lifting it up. He touched his nose to my wrist and inhaled. It was ticklish and I tried to pull away, but his grip was firm. I was going nowhere unless he said so.

Without speaking, his twisted my hand in his grip, bringing my thumb up to his mouth. He slipped it inside and I had a moment to register the damp warmth before a sharp burning pain raked across my thumb pad.

I gasped, yanking harder, but every muscle in Vall's body tensed at the same time. He growled, actually growled, and then I was yanked right into him, his head bent low as his mouth sought my throat.

Remembering what had happened to the four-starred woman, I started struggling, thrashing against him, trying to keep my skin—and my blood—away from the sharpness of his teeth.

"Shhh." I heard. "Shhh." I realized dimly that he was trying to soothe me. It didn't help—I was too tense, braced for the pain, but instead of teeth, I felt the heat of a tongue sliding up the cords of my neck. Just when I thought I might snap from the tension of waiting, he stepped back. I stared at him, eyes wide, but he was looking at Rin. He looked satisfied.

No, he looked absolutely delighted.

"I will take her," he said.

CHAPTER FIVE

It was hard to think around the roaring in his head. Vall held on tight to the little tribute, who looked ready to bolt at the slightest opportunity, and tried to calm his whirling thoughts.

He'd been furious when he'd arrived for the challenges and found the floor empty of males, but the fools obviously hadn't taken the time to question why a starless female would be so vibrant with health, had passed right over the treasure he held in his hands.

A sip, the tiniest sip, that was all he'd taken, but Vall could feel the heat of it pulsing round his whole body. He'd drunk from a four-star female once, when he'd been grievously injured, his life hanging by a thread, and it had been nothing like that. Which meant—and it was insane to think it, but Vall didn't have any other answer—the female who was now his must have even purer blood. Five stars. It was unfathomable, there wasn't a five-star thrall on the planet that he knew of, but there was no other explanation.

More. He wanted more. Wanted to crush her to him and pierce the thin tissue of her skin with his teeth and let the blood flow down his throat in a gush. The dragon in his chest stirred, eager at the thought, already starving for another taste of her, but Vall forced it back into submission. Now was not the time. He needed to take his female and run before any other bastard came along and tried to take her from him.

"Come," he said, tugging at her with gentle pressure. She was a tiny little thing compared to him, the bones of her wrist fragile enough to break with a single squeeze.

Fragile she might be, and the scent of her fear in the air was enough to burn Vall's nostrils, but she was determined, digging her heels in and leaning back against his grip.

"No, wait. I can't go with you!"

The dragon inside him didn't like that. A growl ripped out of Vall's throat.

She stilled at the noise, eyes widening, and he used the moment to pull her off balance. She came crashing into his chest with a startled yelp. Before she could try to pull back, to escape, he had her scooped up in his arms.

"Settle," he snarled when she wriggled hard.

The firm approach seemed to work, because she stopped trying to escape his hold and stared up at him, panting softly. Satisfied she was done challenging him—for now, at least— he nodded once at the Administrator and walked out.

Finn was waiting for him just outside the challenge arena. His worried expression turned to one of relief when he saw Vall emerge, a thrall in his arms, but that dimmed when he looked to her cheek.

"She's unmarked," he commented.

"I'll explain once we get out of here." He wanted to get her back to the pack den, wanted her cosseted away and protected. Then he could take a little time to work out who she was, where she came from and why the fuck one drop of her blood set fire to him the way it had.

Finn didn't ask any more questions, just got moving, leading Vall and his precious bundle back out into the sunshine, where Jay and Lyne were waiting with the hover vehicle. Immediately, Vall felt the beast inside him quiet down. The full pack would be enough to protect her.

"You got one!" Jay exclaimed, grinning. Then he, too, latched onto her unmarked cheek and his face fell. "She's—"

"Get the hover going," Vall snarled. He stepped up onto the rear of the vehicle, then strode to the front, taking the seat just behind where Jay was fumbling with the controls, his shoulders hunched against Vall's obvious displeasure.

Finn took the seat beside him, leaning over to look at the female in Vall's arms.

He resisted the urge to twist away and hide her from view — she was the pack's thrall, her blood the key to keeping them in peak condition to fight. They'd shared multiple thralls before, the females serving for five years before being *retired* to live out a life of luxury, a gift for their sacrifice. This was different though. A voice within Vall was whispering *mine*.

Ours, he told himself firmly.

"She's not marked." Finn repeated his previous words, waiting respectfully.

"She hasn't been tested," Vall told him, raising his voice enough that Jay and Lyne would hear him over the rumble of the hover vehicle as it took off, getting them out of the city and towards their more private — more secure — pack den.

"How can that be?" Finn asked. "Every female is tested at birth."

"Not this one."

Vall looked down at the female, who gazed back, her naked cheeks bleached white. The fingers gripping his arms were bloodless, blunted nails digging into his flesh. She was scared, he realized shamefully, and he bent his head to nuzzle at the top of her head.

"What's her name?" Finn asked. Vall's shame doubled as he realized he didn't know.

"Little one," he murmured softly. "What are you called?"

She transferred her gaze from Finn to him, the dragon inside instantly preening, wanting to impress her.

It took her two attempts to get her name out. "Lana," she whispered.

Lana. Lana Ridian. Lana Mate, because after just a single

drop of blood, he realized he never planned to let her go. Unable to resist, he lifted her hand back up to his mouth and licked at the tiny wound he'd inflicted on her thumb. She whimpered, afraid, and he stroked her hair as he shifted his focus to her wrist. He couldn't resist. His mouth was watering, his pulse thundering in anticipation of the blood that would soon be coursing through his veins.

As gently as he could, he let his teeth melt through her pale skin. The blood flowed thickly, hot and tinged with a metallic taste that made Vall groan as he fastened down harder.

There it was, that same ecstasy. A fire in his veins, it rolled through him, unmaking and remaking him as it went, making his muscles sing with strength and his cock harden like a rock in his trousers.

He could have kept drinking from her forever, reveling in the rapture that was like a full-body orgasm, but his dragon sensed her tension, her fear, and pulled back, demanding he comfort her. He lapped at the wound, encouraging it to seal, then wrapped his arms around her.

"It's all right," he murmured, because he could feel her trembling, could hear her frightened little gasps. "It's all right."

"Vall," Finn muttered, his ears shifting back with uncertainty as he stared at Vall. "Your eyes. They're glowing."

Vall felt it then, the dragon unfurling in his chest, stretching as it filled his entire body. His breath left his body in a rush as he realized his skin was tingling, buzzing, ready to dissolve and reform if he just willed it.

"I think I could transform," he said quietly. "I think I could fully shift."

Utter silence met this statement, the rest of the pack staring at him with astonishment and then down to the female in his arms with undisguised envy. Though it made him want to growl, to let the dragon out so it could snap and snarl and warn the others away, Vall let them look their fill. They were a pack, a family, and if it was true that Lana's blood was the key to releasing the dragon that had been trapped within his people for half a millennium, then perhaps she could unleash them all.

He looked down at her, her strange rounded pupils reduced to pinpricks and her lips bloodless. She was cold, he realized suddenly, though it was a hot day, the sun beating down on them.

"Lana," he murmured, jostling her gently. Her gaze jumped to his, but there was no hint of recognition there. No echo of the joy that he felt, or even nervousness. Fear. There was nothing but emptiness.

"Lyne," he roared, though his pack member was only feet away and would have heard him if he'd whispered.

Lyne was in front of him quickly, nudging out Finn out of the way so that he could settle at Vall's feet. Vall knew Lynne had been on tenterhooks, waiting desperately for permission to approach.

"Something's wrong with her," he told him. Lyne might be bottom of their pack in terms of dominance, but he had the most medical knowledge, was responsible for patching them up whenever they were injured during engagements. "Fix her."

Lyne flinched at the command in Vall's voice, but his hands were steady as he pressed them to her forehead and felt at the pulse point on her neck.

"I think she's in shock," he said a moment later. "How much did you take from her?"

He raised his gaze up to meet Vall's for the space of a heartbeat, but it was long enough for Vall to see the hint of censure in them.

"Hardly any," he bit back defensively. "A few mouthfuls at most. It cannot be that."

"It could be trauma," Lyne offered, his hand pressed to her cheek in a lingering caress Vall wanted to fix by ripping his medic's arm off. "I can smell her fear."

So could Vall. He'd been able to scent it since the first moment he'd touched her, though it had intensified since then, but he hadn't really thought anything of it. He'd dismissed it as the natural apprehension of a female faced with a new aggressive male.

"What do I do?" he demanded, shame lending his words a hard edge.

Lyne sat back on his heels, expression thoughtful. "If it were one of us, I'd suggest an infusion from a thrall."

"You think we should find another female for her to drink from?" Vall snapped, agitated.

"No." This time Lyne held Vall's gaze. "I'm suggesting you let her drink from you."

Everything within Vall stood up to attention at that, his dragon intrigued, excited even. *Yes*, it whispered to him, *have her take us into her. Let our blood flow in her veins.* It was a hotly possessive thought, and Vall didn't even try to temper it. He lifted his thumb and tore open the pad with his teeth, blood spurting up freely. He held it up to Lana, but she twisted away, struggling feebly in his arms.

"No," he murmured. "Take it."

Grabbing hold of her jaw, he steadied her and shoved his thumb past her blunt little teeth. She tried to jerk her head away, and when she couldn't, attempted to thrust his digit out of her mouth with her tongue. He felt it rasp over his flesh, smooth and slick and warm, and his erection, which had dissipated slightly with worry, surged anew.

"Suck," he said, leaning down to murmur the word into her ear. "Drink. Just a little. It will help, I promise."

It had better. If it didn't, he was going to wring Lyne's neck.

Just when he thought he was going to have to pinch her

nostrils together, cut off her air to force her to comply, she swallowed.

"That's it," he encouraged. "Just a little more."

This time she obeyed, that hot little tongue raking over his flesh and making his eyes roll back in his head, his balls throb beneath his engorged shaft.

When she released his thumb with a wet little plop, he wanted to push her to take more, but she was panting and gasping, shifting restlessly on his lap. Her head fell back onto his shoulder and he was relieved to see that her cheeks were now warm with color, her eyelids fluttering, as if she wanted to open her eyes but couldn't. He was about to grab Lyne by the throat and demand to know what the hell was wrong with her now when she gave a soft little moan. Her thighs parted and the most mouth-watering scent slid up from between her legs.

Gods, she was aroused. More than aroused. Her fingers pressed against the muscles of his chest as she squirmed, those sexy little gasps punctuated by moans. He slipped his hand between her cloth-covered legs and felt her thigh muscles trembling. Shifting slightly higher, he had a moment to luxuriate in the heat of her before she tensed, then started rubbing at his hand. She was coming, he realized, orgasming in one long roll that had her head thrashing in denial even as she rode against the pressure of his fingers.

"Please," she pleaded. "Please, please, please."

"I am here," he promised. "I have you."

She gave a sudden keening wail, her body tensing all over, before slumping down against him. Vall waited for her eyes to open. When they didn't, he reached up and pressed a palm to her forehead. She gave a little mewl at his touch, nestling closer, but she remained unconscious, her breathing deep and even.

"Is she all right?" Jay called from the controls of the hover vehicle. Concern was writ all over his face, but his eyes were black with lust, his nostrils flared.

"Just get us home," Vall growled. "Now."

CHAPTER SIX

When I opened my eyes, I wasn't in the strange vehicle anymore. I was lying on a bed in a dimly lit room, a silky soft fur covering my body. I had a brief moment of panic before I realized that I was still wearing my coral-colored outfit. I wriggled a bit, enjoying the soft mattress and pillows that seemed to be bracketing my body at every angle, then winced as I felt a slight dampness between my legs. I hadn't imagined that, then.

"You're awake." The growl came from beyond the bed and startled me into emitting a small, undignified squeak.

I contemplated hiding under the covers, but whoever was sitting there wasn't likely to just go away. Cautiously, the fur pulled up protectively beneath my chin, I sat up.

There he was, the warrior who had barged in late to the challenges and had to take me home as the booby prize. What had Rin called him? Vall. Vall Ridian. He looked smaller, folded down onto a small stool just beyond the confines of the large bed, but that illusion faded when he stood up and took the two small steps needed to reach the edge of the mattress. He reached a hand out and rested it on the bed, stroking the edges of my fur cover as if he was stroking me. I resisted the urge to twitch it out of his hands and the even stronger urge that said I should stick one of my body parts there instead. Quite a few of them seemed eager to volunteer for the job.

What had happened on the journey here was still a tangle in my mind. I'd gone from being kidnapped — claimed — by one warrior, to being surrounded by four of them. Self-preservation made me retreat in on myself, like a mouse that thinks if it freezes perhaps the large, hungry cat won't notice it. Then Vall had taken my wrist and bit into it. Like an honest-to-god vampire, he'd drunk my blood and I'd felt his cock harden beneath me where I sat on his lap. That had been a bit much for my tiny little brain, and I think I'd been well on my way to having a nervous breakdown when he shoved his thumb into my mouth. I tasted the blood straight away and I tried to spit it out, but he was so much bigger than me, so much stronger. I swallowed the blood and then . . .

And then it was like a rush of heat all through my body. I felt as if someone had set my veins on fire. My pulse was pounding—and so were other places. An orgasm the likes of which I'd never experienced powered through me and then just kept on going. Dear God, I rode the hand of a total stranger.

Mortified, I kept my gaze off his face and on his magical fingers. I felt like I should apologize, but I also really wanted to ask if I could suck on his thumb again. Instead, I decided silence was the better part of valor and kept my mouth firmly shut.

"Are you well?" he asked quietly.

I nodded, because being claimed against my will aside, I felt better than I had in years. I felt alive, my limbs singing with strength and my thoughts sharp. But I also felt apprehensive and out of place and very confused about what the hell was going on.

"Where am I?" I asked.

"My home," he replied. "The pack den." Then he gave a small, hopeful smile. "Your home."

Right. I decided just to leave that there.

"The pack?" There had been three other men in the vehicle—who had *witnessed* my wanton little sex show, I thought, cringing—but they were nowhere to be seen now. It was just me and Vall in the room, the doorless exit showing no one lingering in the hallway, either.

He paused. "What do you know of us, Lana?"

"I don't even know what planet I'm on," I answered honestly. The improbable opportunity to use that phrase literally for once had a laugh twitching at my lips, but it didn't last long, because it was true — I had absolutely no idea where I was. And, as Rin had so helpfully pointed out, no way to get home.

He blinked, his expression somber. "You said you were not supposed to be a tribute, I did not really understand . . ." He tailed off.

It was on the tip of my tongue to tell him that he didn't try to understand, that he was too busy sampling my blood and then striding out with me up in his arms like a sack of potatoes, but I held it in.

"You are on Trinia. We are Triniuns, the dominant race on this planet. We have evolved into different, well, I suppose if we were animals, you would say breeds. Clans is the word we use. The same species, but our differences have become marked. Those who are weak physically but strong in organization become Administrators, running our governments and such. There are also Artists and Thinkers. Those who are physically strong, like me, are part of the Warrior clan. The dragon is powerful in us and we are bred for fighting and protecting. We live in packs, and to satiate the dragon we have thralls — "

"That would be me?" I asked.

He nodded. "Thralls provide blood to the Warriors in their pack, keeping them strong and keeping the dragon sated."

"You keep mentioning dragons," I pointed out.

The look he levelled at me was intense. I held it for a moment, then glanced away, peering down the hallway where I thought I saw a shadow shifting. Maybe the rest of Vall's pack were lingering nearby after all.

"Our ancestors were able to become fully formed drag-ons — shift their shape and take to the skies. But the blood of our females has become diluted, we're not sure how, and as that happened, we lost the ability to transform."

"So." I licked my lips and thought about what he said. "You expect me to donate blood to you and the rest of your pack? Are there more of you than the ones I . . .met" — and had an incredible, mind-blowing orgasm in front of — "ear-lier?"

"No." He shook his head. "There are only the four of us."

Well, that was a relief. Sort of. At least I wasn't expected to be some sort of communal drink fountain in the playground.

"And the blood you gave me?"

Had I thought the look he gave me before was intense? It was nothing compared to the smoking hot stare he hit me with now.

"You were in shock, I was trying to help you. But yes, that is something shared between mates," he said.

"Mates?" The word came out a squeak.

"You enjoyed it, didn't you?"

"I—"

"I know you did, I could smell it."

If it was possible to go up in flames from embarrassment, I would have done it right then.

"An orgasm doesn't make a marriage," I said desperately. Though, if I'd had a few more, I might have stayed married a little longer.

"Marriage?"

"That's what we call mating where I'm from."

He nodded slowly. "I have yet to prove myself and my pack. I understand."

And my pack? Did that mean what I thought it did? I was afraid to ask.

"For now—" He held out his hand. "I would show you around your new home, introduce you properly to the rest of the pack."

I let him pull me from the safety of the bed and lead me out of the bedroom. I realized as we walked down the hall that the house was carved out of rock, the walls thick and painted a warm cream color, the windows few and far between. What little I could see of outside told me it was pitch dark, giving me no clues as to what the landscape looked like. We could have been on the desert floor or high up on the side of a mountain, I couldn't tell.

Vall pointed out several sleeping chambers, windowless little cells with single beds and none of the sumptuousness of the room I'd woken up in, which had a bed that could comfortably sleep more than two people. I decided to leave that thought well alone, peering into the washroom which had an enormous tub that was more like a swimming pool, already filled, the water lapping gently at the lip. There was no one in the kitchen or dining room that Vall showed me, and I was beginning to wonder if they were hiding from me when we turned a corner and emerged into a large living space complete with a big open air balcony, a large stone fireplace and three Warriors lounging on an enormous and comfortable looking corner sofa.

They jumped to their feet as soon as we appeared, curious gazes fixed on me. I went from face to face, vaguely recognizing them from the journey here and acutely aware that the last time they'd seen me I'd been in the throes of the most exquisite ecstasy.

"Lana," Vall said, his grip on my hand tugging me fully into the room where I would have lingered awkwardly in the entryway. "This is my pack. My second, Finn." One of the Warriors, who was even taller than Vall though slightly less thick with muscle, nodded solemnly at me. "Jay." This one gave me a wide grin, drinking me in as he waved. I offered him a small smile in return, and the grin widened impossibly further. "And Lyne." Lyne was small and stocky, a scar bisecting one eye. They all had the same dark skin, hints of blue glittering where the light from scones on the wall bounced off them, but Lyne was the only one not to have matching black hair. His was a light grey that he had pulled back tightly into a ponytail.

"Hello," I said awkwardly, when the silence had gone on long enough for it to be clear they were waiting on me to say something. "I . . .It's nice to meet you, properly this time."

"I enjoyed our first meeting," Jay quipped, eyes gleaming as he smirked.

My face flamed at the same time as Vall emitted a low growl that sent all the hairs rising on the back of my neck. Jay's face fell and so did his gaze, drilling a hole into the flagstoned floor.

"I apologize, Alpha," he mumbled.

Vall's growl receded, but he also let go of my hand and reached up to grip my neck in what was clearly a claiming, even to me.

There was food on the coffee table in front of the sofa, I noticed, as Vall led me over to sit down. I hadn't eaten since breakfast this morning, a long, *long* time ago, skipping lunch and dinner to try and get that stupid woman's cake ready on time, and my stomach twisted, looking at the simple array of bread and dried meat and fruits.

"Are you hungry?" Vall asked, noting my fixed look.

I nodded, and the next thing I knew he'd grabbed a plate and piled it high. He sat beside me on the couch, offering a bite of bread torn from the loaf and dipped in something the pink of jam but the consistency of honey. I tried to take it from him, but he pulled it away until I gave up and let him feed me. The bread was soft and tasty, though more yeasty than I was used to, and the odd pink stuff had a tart, slightly bitter aftertaste. I wasn't keen, but I was too hungry to be fussy. The bread was followed by slivers of gamey meat and small fruits, all delivered by Vall's hand.

"I can feed myself," I objected at one point, a drop of juice from a fruit that was too big to be consumed in one bite running down my chin. Vall didn't say anything, just kept looking at me with that intense gaze of his, holding the morsel away until I stopped reaching for it. The rest of the pack watched in silence, making me feel like I was at the center of another erotic display — albeit a bit tamer. Finally, when I'd eaten as much as my stomach could handle, my mouth cracked open into a jaw-splitting yawn. I didn't know how long I'd been unconscious for earlier, but it wasn't long enough. My body was exhausted and my mind was crying out for an opportunity to shut down and process for a while.

"You can sleep soon," Vall promised, fingers gentle on my face as he swept my hair back behind my ear. "There is one more thing we must do first."

He tugged me off the sofa and led me over to stand in front of the large fireplace. It was big enough that I could have comfortably crawled inside it, the fire blazing there fed by enormous chunks of wood. It wasn't until he clasped both my hands in his and went down on one knee, the rest of the pack in a semi-circle behind him, that I realized we were about to perform some sort of ceremony.

He was so tall that there was very little difference in our heights with him kneeling like this. I barely had to tilt my head to look down into his eyes, staring up at mine with an expression of fierce joy.

"Lana," he said, his voice lower and gruffer than I'd become accustomed to. "I thank you for the honor you do me, offering your blood as my thrall. I promise to protect you and keep you safe, to see to your comfort and to respect you as is your due."

He pulled my hands towards him and I went, thinking he was going to kiss my knuckles. Instead, he nipped at one of my fingertips, drawing blood. I bit my tongue to hold in my yelp and watched as he closed his eyes briefly and shuddered, an expression of ecstasy on his face. When he opened his eyes again, they were shining a brighter shade of silver. I blinked, feeling like there was someone else entirely looking out at me from behind his gaze, but a moment later it was gone. Stiffly, he climbed to his feet, both hands cupping my face gently before he let me go and stood to the side.

Finn approached next, taking up the same position on his knees in front of me. He held out his hands for mine and I hesitated briefly, understanding what was happening this time. I wasn't sure I wanted to get chewed on by three more Warriors.

"Do you offer me your blood, Lana?" he asked softly. There was something in his expression, hope warring with fear of rejection, that tugged at my heartstrings and made me place my hands in his. I listened as he repeated the same words Vall had said and then braced, waiting for the sharp sting of teeth piecing my flesh. Instead, he placed a soft kiss on each of my fingertips, and when he pulled my left index finger into his mouth and drew on it, I didn't even feel the burn. I saw it, though, when my blood hit his tongue. His pupils dilated, the soft blue color of his eyes swirling cobalt bright. His gentle grip on my hands became bruising tight for an instant before he made himself let go.

"Forgive me, Lana," he said. "I thought I was prepared, but I was not." His gaze turned to Vall, standing at my shoulder. "You are right, I feel it too."

I didn't get a chance to ask him to explain that cryptic comment, because as soon as he rose, Jay took his place. He didn't wait for permission, grabbing both of my hands out of the air and holding them against the heat of his chest.

"Beautiful Lana," he began. "I thank you for the honor of your blood. I swear I will protect you and keep you safe, see to your comfort and to respect you." He sent me a wickedly hot look, lifting my hands until his breath feathered over my skin. "I cannot wait to taste you," he murmured.

He wasn't as gentle as Finn, the rasp of his canines making me wince, but the way he dragged his tongue slowly along the length of my finger, licking up the tiny dribble of blood that had slid free, made me shiver. I also couldn't complain about the way he made no bones about how it made him feel, giving a little groan before he got to his feet, his erection tenting the front of his trousers.

Then there was just Lyne left. He came forward slowly, glancing at me for permission before he'd even lowered to his knees in front of me, then keeping his gaze fixed on the floor when he got there. His hands were clenched in fists down by his side, and at first I thought maybe he didn't want to take my blood, but then I saw him take a deep breath and look up at me. Like Finn, he held his hands out to me, waiting for me to take them. I did, and then impulsively I leaned down and kissed him softly on the cheek. I don't know what made me do it, but the smile he gave me afterwards was beatific.

"I thank you for the honor you do me, offering your blood as thrall," he said, as formal as Vall had been. He tripped over the second half of the vow, his gaze fixed on my hands, on the bloodied wounds I'd collected on three fingertips and my wrist—and of course, the thumb Vall had pricked earlier when he'd chosen me. I was amassing quite the array of tiny injuries and beginning to feel like a pincushion.

Ignoring my remaining unblemished fingers, he took one hand and turned it so that the gash on the inside of my wrist was revealed, the skin just beginning to scab over. Gently, he scraped at it with one razor sharp tooth, irritating the wound just enough for a few beads of bloods to spring free. His tongue flicked out and lapped at them before he placed a soft kiss there. "Thank you," he repeated.

He remained there on his knees, looking up at me with something uncomfortably like adoration, until Vall stepped forward and drew me back against him.

"Rest," he murmured into my ear. "It's time for you to rest now."

I twisted my head so that I could see him out of the corner of my eye.

"Alone?" I asked, one eyebrow raised.

He took a moment to answer. "We won't leave you alone, not even in the safety of the den, but it is yours to command who sleeps in your bed."

"*I* do," I said firmly.

I let Vall lead me back to the bedroom and tried to ignore the softly spoken *For now* that I would I have bet my life came from Jay.

CHAPTER SEVEN

There was a crack on my bedroom ceiling that I'd been slowly watching crawl to the central light fixture over the course of the last year. When I woke up and stared up at the ceiling above me, made of stone and not the ageing Artex slapped on almost every surface of my run-down condo, I missed that crack. I'd been fretting about it ever since it appeared, knowing I didn't have the money in my bank account to fix it if it was more than the simplest repair job, but it was also on my ceiling, in my home, scrimped and scraped for after my husband fought for every penny in our divorce. In a strange way, I was proud of that crack.

Now my condo was gone, as was my whole life. I hadn't really given much thought to it, but I wondered now what had happened after the crash. Was my body there, broken and bleeding, mangled up in the remains of my car? Or when the police and paramedics arrived, had someone clambered down the long grass, peered inside and just seen an empty seat? Was I a horrible memory for someone, or an intriguing mystery?

I'd probably never find out.

I tried to breathe against the swell of emotion that rose up in my throat at the thought of my friends, my family, my business that I'd worked so hard to get off the ground, all gone. I should be gone, too. I was trying hard to be grateful that I wasn't, to be happy that I'd been given this bizarre second chance, but it wasn't easy.

A whole new world. New people, new customs. Instead of

making cakes, I was going to be a blood bank for a pack of Warriors with a dragon inside them, even if it was dormant. It was . . .a big change. I wasn't sure that I was ready for it, but going back wasn't an option, and I was glad to be *some-where* rather than nowhere. I wasn't a religious person, hadn't been to church in more than twenty years save weddings and funerals, so I'd expected to just wink out of existence when I died.

This was definitely better than that.

Resolved to make the best of things, I rolled up and to the side, dangling my legs over the edge of the bed, and froze. Vall was there, sitting on a low stool against the wall opposite. Except for the fact he had his head back and his eyes closed, he was in the exact same position he'd taken up when I'd lain down to sleep last night. Had he spent the whole night there like that?

I didn't want to wake him up—although he didn't look at all comfortable—so I eased quietly down off the bed, my thoughts on my pressing need to visit the luxurious bath-room. As soon as my feet touched the ground, though, Vall's eyes snapped open.

"You're awake," he said.

I nodded, grimacing a little uncomfortably. Aware that I wasn't wearing a bra, I crossed my arms over my chest, hands rubbing at my upper arms even though I wasn't cold. I stopped abruptly, feeling a pull on my wrist and remember-ing the cuts on my fingertips from the strange ceremony last night, but when I shifted my hands to look at them, there were no signs of the bite marks. The skin was unblemished, there weren't even any red marks to tell me which fingers it had been. Even the wound on my wrist, which had been much deeper, was now little more than a pale pink mark, the skin slightly shiny and new looking.

I hadn't imagined it, had I?

Leaning forwards, Vall took my hands, looking at me questioningly.

"The bite marks," I blurted. "They're gone."

"You didn't expect them to be?" he asked, confused. "They were only scratches."

"They were deep enough to draw blood," I argued. That, after all, had been the point of them.

Vall tilted his head, a small frown wrinkling his forehead. "You do not heal when your skin is cut?"

"Well, yeah," I said, a little defensively. "But not that quickly."

"You took some of my blood," he suggested, the comment offhand, but my face flaming red as I remembered just what had happened right after I'd swallowed it. "Perhaps it has helped you heal more like my people do."

Orgasms and healing power. If I could bottle their blood and take it back to Earth, I'd make a fortune.

Vall led me through to the bathroom and left me to tend to my personal business. After I'd finished, I started eyeing up the tub. I'd already dipped my hand in it to ascertain that it was the perfect temperature for bathing—warm, but not too hot—and I felt grimy, my skin itching to be clean, but I was also in a house with four strange men and I wasn't sure I wanted to start stripping my kit off. There was no lock on the door.

I was still warring with myself when the door abruptly flew open. Finn walked in, a handful of clothes in his hands. He stopped short when he saw me just standing there, awkward in the middle of room.

"Vall said you were bathing," he said, gaze flitting to the tub and back. He took in my fully clothed state, my bone-dry hair. "You are finished?"

"I . . .well, no. I wasn't sure—" I gave up explaining and offered a helpless little shrug.

"I've brought clothes for you to change into." He made a face. "I am sorry, they are from our last thrall. We will take you shopping for your own things as soon as we are able."

"I'm sure they're fine," I replied lamely, watching as he put them down on a padded bench.

"There are drying cloths here too," he told me, pressing on a discreet pressure point in the wall so that a door swung open, revealing shelves with towels.

"Right. Great. Thanks."

I fiddled with the hem of my tunic but didn't make any move to lift it up over my head. Finn was still there, lingering by the towel cupboard.

"Do you require help with your bath?" he asked, voice husky and expression hopeful.

It was like one of those laughable fantasies, the prelude to a sexy romp in the water, but I was nothing like the women in those stories. Instead of batting come-and-get-me eye-lashes, I blushed and squirmed. "No, thank you," I managed to get out.

He didn't try to hide his disappointment. "Maybe next time."

I blew out a breath once I was alone in the bathroom again and then, feeling seven times a fool, I slid the bench across the floor until it blocked the door. It wasn't particularly heavy and it likely wouldn't stop anyone determined to come in, but at least it would give me a moment's warning.

The water felt as good as I'd imagined it would. It was hard to relax, though, my attention constantly going back to the door, which thankfully remained closed. I took a moment to just float after I'd scrubbed myself all over. Grief over the sudden ending to my real life threatened to overtake me again, but I willed it back, thinking instead about what might have happened if I'd taken Finn up on his offer.

He was alien, there was no getting around that. Between

his blue-tinged dark skin and the pointy ears — not to mention the small details like the slitted pupils or lack of eyebrows — he was obviously different, but for all that, he looked pretty much like a human male. He certainly had a better body than my ex-husband, or any of my boyfriends, actually. His muscles were sleek but well-defined under his skin and he had broad shoulders, a long, lean figure. He'd be way out of my league back home.

Closing my eyes, I imagined lifting my shirt up and over my head, watching him stalk towards me as I nudged my trousers over the curve of my hip and just let them slide to the floor. He'd be gentle, I thought, picking me up and depositing me in the water, hands running over my scalp as he washed my hair, tickling my skin with light, sensual touches as he soaped up my body.

Of their own accord, my hands slid over my body, one lifting to pinch and flick at my nipples while the fingers of my other went straight between my legs to slide over my clit. I continued the fantasy, Finn kissing my neck as he parted my thighs to wrap them round his waist, his cock nudging at my entrance.

It was my moan that brought me back to myself, the sound amplified in the acoustics of the room. I jack-knifed in the water, sinking down until my chin rested on the surface and staring around guiltily. The room was still empty, the bench blocking the door like I'd left it. My clit was pulsing in time with my pounding heart, demanding I return to what I was doing and finish the job, but I was too worried I might be caught, not sure how many minutes had passed since Finn left me.

Wanting to be out and dressed before anyone came to check whether I'd drowned, I quickly washed away evidence of my arousal and clambered out. After drying myself off, I dived into the clothes Finn had brought for me — a stretchy pair of leggings that I had to fold back at the ankles to reveal my feet and a pretty lilac colored tunic that was a bit tight through the chest but flared out down to my knees until it was really more of a dress—and then attempted to deal with my hair. I found something resembling a comb in a niche beside the bathing tub and manage to wrestle out the tangles then tame the whole thing back into a braid, though I'd nothing to tie it with.

That done, there was nothing left but to go out there and face the music, or, more specifically, the four alien Warriors who wanted to drink my blood to feed their inner dragons.

No problem.

I made it as far as dragging the bench out of the way and opening the door before I got cold feet, an embarrassed squeak coming out when I realized Finn was standing right outside, his back to the bathroom. He turned to look at me, wicked amusement in his eyes and I realized he must have heard me moving the bench back across the floor.

"You don't have to barricade yourself in," he told me. "You're safe here."

"I'm used to a lock on the bathroom door," I said, with all the dignity I could muster.

Finn's eyes darkened slightly. "There are no locks here. We would not be able to get to you if you needed our help. If you wish for privacy, simply ask for it."

"Noted," I said, even more mortified now. I looked beyond him down the hallway. "What happens now?"

"Now we feed you breakfast," Finn said simply.

Unlike the meal Vall fed me the night before, breakfast was eaten in the kitchen, a table and chairs arranged beneath a large window that allowed me to finally see where we were. Finn made me a bowl of a something very similar to porridge, dried fruits dotted here and there, while I gazed at my surroundings. We were high up, that was the first thing to register. The house must be built into the side of a mountain or something, because the ground dropped away steeply to reveal a flat basin of a valley, what looked like a city far off in the distance. I couldn't see any neighbors, the land close by tightly hemmed in by trees, jutting rock formations and flowering plants. There was a flat, roughly circular landing pad, the hover vehicle parked there, and then, if I craned my neck to the right, I was just able to glimpse a second flat area, slightly larger and cleared of vegetation. A small path connected it to the house, though the angle of the building cut off exactly where it ended.

Vall, Jay and Lyne were down there, Jay and Lyne doing their best to knock lumps out of Vall with large sticks shaped roughly like baseball bats. Finn came over and dropped my bowl in front of me, peering out of the window over my shoulder.

"What are they doing?" I asked.

"Training," he said simply.

"Training?" I replied. "They look like they're trying to kill each other! Is that fair, two against one? Vall hasn't even got a weapon."

"Vall is a weapon," Finn replied, looking amused. "Finish your food and we can go down at watch, if you like."

I wasn't sure whether I wanted to get up close and personal to three men bashing the living hell out of each other, but I found myself nodding. I was comfortable enough, here with Finn. I liked him, but as I ate my porridge, my gaze kept going back to Vall, down there in the garden. I caught myself watching the way he moved, ducking and weaving as Jay and Lyne tried to land a blow, striking out fast as a cobra as he landed a few of his own.

Finn was right, he was a weapon.

The door to the training area, I discovered, was hidden in a discreet alcove behind the enormous fireplace in the living area. We went down a steep set of stairs, natural rock hemming us in on both sides, then Finn opened a heavy looking door onto the little gravel path I'd seen from the window. From here, we could already see the three Warriors. They'd stopped fighting and were drinking from water bottles, sweat glistening on their skin.

Vall's head whipped in our direction as soon as we stepped out onto the path. I felt it again, that strange pull to him. It throbbed in my chest, causing me to grind to a halt even though I wanted to run towards him. This thing, this magnetism, it felt alien. It was *in* me but I felt somehow that it wasn't me. Or hadn't been me. It was confusing, but also irresistible, and after a moment I gave in and let it tug me towards Vall, since that was where I wanted to go anyway.

"Lana," he murmured as soon as I was close. His voice saying my name made everything inside me sit up and pay attention.

"Are you well? Have you eaten?"

I nodded, but Vall looked over my head to Finn for confirmation.

I turned just in time to see him finish giving an identical nod.

"She wanted to come down and see you train." His lips twitched. "She was concerned that you were being unfairly treated, outnumbered and weaponless."

"I am a weapon," Vall growled, affronted.

I smiled, breathing out a small laugh. "That's what Finn said."

That mollified Vall, who stepped closer and placed a hand on my waist, sharp claws pricking slightly against my side.

"More faith, please, little Lana. Your mate is a strong Warrior."

There it was again, that word. Mate. My smile became slightly fixed, but the words to deny it, deny him, wouldn't come. He liked that, I could tell. Squeezing my side gently, careful not to cause me even the slightest twinge of pain with his lethal claws, he looked to Finn again.

"I was right, I am stronger. Much stronger. The dragon won't come, not yet, but it's restless." He looked to me. "Her blood is pure, I'd stake my life on it. I feel like I could take on a full nest of sabers by myself." He leaned ever so slightly into me and breathed deeply, like he was drawing my very essence into his lungs. "And I've only had a couple of little sips."

"Well, let's not test that out just yet," Finn said dryly. "How about we try you on three to one, see how you do with that?"

Vall grinned, smug. "I'll wipe the floor with you."

"So you say."

Finn left my side and went to stand by Jay and Lyne, picking up an extra bat.

Vall picked me up, depositing me safely out of the training circle on a large boulder. He stared into my eyes for a long, intense moment, then surprised me by pressing his mouth hard to mine, claiming a fierce kiss. Then he turned and approached the rest of the pack, muscles in his back flexing. With barely a moment to prepare, he launched himself at them, knocking Jay's feet out from under him and disarming Finn with a vicious jab to his forearm.

I sat on my rock, basking in the sunshine, the wide bowl of the valley spread out in the distance and watched four Warriors attempt to kill each other, wide grins on all their faces and muscles gleaming with sweat.

It wasn't a bad view, I thought. Not too bad at all.

CHAPTER EIGHT

I dreamed of dragons.

They soared up above me, majestic, with long, slender necks and strong wings, tails lashing as they rode the currents. I stood on the ground, neck craned and watched them, wishing with all my heart that I could soar too. I reached up to the sky, and one of the dragons immediately detached from the group and swooped down to land in front of me. Enormous nostrils whuffed at my hair, then a head ducked down into my vision, mercury silver eyes the size of dinner plates peering into mine.

When I woke, it was to gaze into that same silver in a man's eyes. Vall squatted just beside the bed.

"You were dreaming," he murmured. "I noticed you tossing and turning and wondered if it was a nightmare."

I thought about the beauty of the dragons, their sleek, lithe movements as they twisted in the sky, the way the sun glinted off their scales and shook my head. "It was a good dream," I said.

He nodded, satisfied and rolled up from the crouch he'd been hunkered down in, sitting on the edge of the bed.

"I thought I decided who was in my bed," I teased.

The look he turned on me was molten. "You're not asleep anymore," he murmured.

I stared up at him, and I couldn't help it. I thought about that first day, about the feeling that rushed through me when his blood hit my system. Like a junkie looking for a fix, I wanted to feel it again, the area between my legs giving a throb of remembered pleasure and my nipples tightening. Vall took a breath, then he paused for a millisecond before taking another, deeper one. He groaned, a sound that slipped into a low growl that definitely wasn't human. He rolled onto the bed, stopping when he came up against my outstretched hand.

I held him there, off balance, his expression hungry and gaze fixed on mine, waiting for permission. I could push at him, I knew—and I wouldn't have to push very hard—and he'd roll away again, take himself up and off the bed. I don't know why I was so sure about that—I'd known him for less than a day, and yet I was.

I didn't want to push him away, though. Slowly, nervously, I scooted back in the bed, making more space for him. He followed, shifting across and up until he was leaning on one elbow, looking down at me where I lay flat on my back. I gazed up at him, hand reaching to stroke down his jaw, which was smooth and hairless, not even the finest hairs catching on my fingertips and he dropped down to nuzzle at my neck.

The quick action froze me, a bolt of fear making me brace against the anticipated pain of his sharp teeth, but he only nipped and licked, setting my nerves on fire. His free hand tugged the fur covering off my body, exposing the thin slip I'd been given to wear to bed. It was a study, cotton-like material, clearly made for someone a bit taller and, unfortunately, slimmer than me. It trapped my breasts and tangled round my legs, but it had been better than going to bed naked in a strange house with strange men, so I'd donned it gratefully.

Now, though, it was in the way of Vall touching me, which I desperately wanted. Not a drop of his blood was running in my veins, but my heart was still pounding, my legs restless. He was big, he was muscular, and the strange little growls he was emitting deep in his chest as he stroked across my collar bones and sternum, so, so close to my waiting breasts, were really doing it for me.

"You should be wearing pretty things," he murmured. "Delicate things. So that you can get angry at me when I tear them off you."

Taking hold of the neckline of my nightgown, he ripped it down the middle, exposing my breasts to the air and his roving fingers. He was cruel, running his fingers up the bottom curves and circling around my areola, avoiding the tips entirely as he stroked and stroked and stroked.

"Please," I moaned, shifting against him.

"Please what?"

"Touch me!"

"I am touching you."

I could feel his smile against my neck. "Touch . . .touch my nipples," I ground out, too needy to be embarrassed.

"This?" he asked, scraping across the tip of one with his thumb nail. I cried out, the sensation striking through me like lightning.

"More?" he asked.

"More," I panted and he rewarded me by doing it again, this time to the other side. I whimpered. My breasts had never been particularly sensitive, but he seemed to know how to make them come alive.

He hadn't kissed me yet, not once, but that just made me concentrate more on all the places he was touching me. His mouth was hot at the juncture between my neck and my shoulder. One hand slid up to take a tight grip on my hair and prevent me from shying away from his lips and tongue, his thumb and forefinger as they took my agonizingly sensitive nipple and rolled it before giving it a sharp pinch and a flick.

"Too much," I gasped.

"No it isn't," he disagreed, shifting so that he could move down my body and replace his fingers with his mouth.

At first he concentrated his torment of me there, taking one areola fully into his mouth and sucking deeply while flicking the neglected tip with his thumb, but then he started to slide his hand further down. He moved over my stomach, with its slightly rounded swell and down into the curls between my legs.

"Open for me," he commanded softly, lifting his head to stare at me with those quicksilver eyes. Without hesitation, I shifted my legs wide enough for his fingers to slide all the way down into my wetness. He didn't let me hide, holding my gaze as he ran two fingers along my slit. My clit pulsed, impatient, and I found myself lifting up, searching for his touch.

"Here?" he asked, moving lower and sliding a finger just an inch inside me. That felt good, but it wasn't what I wanted. I shifted my hips again, dislodging him, and he quested up, his fingers separating my labia this time and spreading my arousal up and up until finally, he reached my clit.

I yanked in a short sharp breath, everything strung tight, and he smiled, slow and satisfied.

"This is where you like to be touched, is it? What do you like, I wonder? Little circles?" Slowly, ever so slowly, he traced a circle around my clit. It was unbearable, the sensation making my eyes roll back in my head. I wanted to twitch away from him, but I couldn't move, too focused on the intense pleasure he was wringing from me with such a slow gentle touch. "Or do you like to be stroked?" He pressed down a little harder, fingers finding the side of my hood and rubbing in small motions back and forth.

"Like that!" I gasped. "Please, more! Like that!"

"No." He shook his head before giving my clit two little taps with the pad of his fingers and then returning to those slow, light circles.

I couldn't stand it. The need to come was clawing at me

and I batted his hand away, replacing it with my own fingers and rubbing furiously, just the way I liked. I had a moment for the pleasure to build, eyes widening in anticipation of what was going to be an incredible orgasm, when a growl ripped through my haze of ecstasy and my hand was torn away. Vall slammed it up by my head and then pulled my other up to join it. He held them there, both of my wrists easily encircled by one of his hands, then went right back to what he was doing.

"Spread your legs wider," he instructed. "Be a good little thrall and I'll give you what you want. You want to come, don't you?"

He stopped circling and went back to tap, tap, tapping, each touch sending a jolt of electricity through me. Though it was agony and ecstasy in one, I widened my legs as far as the torn remnants of the nightgown would allow, wanting more of his touch, my clit throbbing with need. When he started circling again, I panted, shaking my head from side to side.

"I can't," I told him. "It's too much."

It was like a razor across my nerves, the pleasure piercing and almost painful in its sharpness. He'd lifted his mouth from my breast, wasn't touching me anywhere but his grip around my wrists and his fingertip around my clit, and I was strung tight as a bow.

"Please!" I begged, when he kept going, round and round and steady and exquisite and just too slow to let me build to orgasm. "Please!"

"All right," he murmured. "Since you asked so nicely."

Changing the angle slightly, he pressed a little harder, circled a little faster, then faster and faster still. All I could do was lie there and pant, legs stretched as wide as I could get them, offering up my pussy to his fingers. The pressure built until I crested the wave, waited breathlessly for it to crash over me.

When my orgasm hit, it thundered through me with suffocating force, rolling my eyes back into my head and making my whole body float for a suspended moment. Electric pleasure skated the razor wire, unfurling in a bloom that touched every part of me. When it all became too much, my muscles jerking and contracting, Vall's hand was suddenly gone, his body positioned over me. I didn't know when he'd removed his trousers, but his cock was there, at my core, ready to push into me. Still stunned by the power of my orgasm, I realized my hands were free to clutch at his arms as he held himself above me.

"Yes!" I gasped. "Now. In me."

Giving a small grunt of acknowledgement, he started to push inside. I was tight, my pelvis still throbbing with delicious contractions, and though I hadn't been given a chance to get my hands on him, I could feel how large he was as he forced swollen tissue to make way for his penetration. He slid in and pulled back, slid in and pulled back. Each time he forged a little deeper, stretched me a little further. I felt possessed, branded, and all I could do was cling to him and chant, "Yes! Please! More!" over and over in a helpless litany.

When he was finally seated fully, he leaned down and kissed me. It was a sensuous melding of tongues and it took me a long, slow moment to understand that he'd used one of his razor-sharp canines to slash a small wound in his tongue, his every thrust and lick transferring blood into my mouth.

"Now," he said, pulling back until just an inch separated our faces. "Come for me again."

He started to move, thrusting deep and hard and rhythmically, just as my body began to explode like fireworks detonating in my veins. I clawed at his arms and shoulders, almost afraid as pleasure crested and broke in a never-ending cycle that didn't let me breathe. Feeling lost in the storm of it, I lifted up and bit at his chin and lower lip until he pinned me down, thrusting into my mouth with his tongue in the same way his cock was surging into my body. That helped ground me and I clung on for the ride as he pounded into me tirelessly.

When he came, it was with a groan and a final thrust, piercing me deep enough that I felt him everywhere inside me. Face pressed to mine, he panted through the tiny aftershocks that rocked his frame, hands stroking my hair and neck and shoulders.

"Mate," he murmured softly. "Mate."

I didn't deny him. A strange feeling was gripping me, one that urged me to press my body to his, to revel in the closeness. When he pulled out and shifted onto his side, I did just that, snuggling into his chest and burrowing closer when his arms wrapped around me. I felt safe and cherished, the steady beat of his heart beneath my ear reassuring and strong.

"Are you well, little one?" he asked a long moment later. "Did I hurt you?"

I shook my head, pulling back far enough that I could look up at him, allow him to see the satisfaction in my face.

"What about you, though?" I asked uncertainty. "You didn't . . .feed."

His eyes flared, that quicksilver burning liquid bright, but he shook his head ever so slightly. "We do not need to feed every day. You would be covered in bites and bruises if we did that. We only truly need to feed when we are deployed on a mission. Anything outside of that is only for pleasure."

Oh boy. If my blood did for them anything close to what Vall's blood did to me, then pleasure wasn't really the word.

"Come," Vall said. "We need to bathe. Today, I would take you to two friends of mine. They are Thinkers and they specialize in trying to understand why the blood of our females is becoming more and more dilute."

"You want to test my blood."

"I want to test your blood," he agreed.

Chapter Nine

Vall left Lana to enjoy the enormous bathing pool, making do with a quick wash under the icy spray of the shower. It was the very last thing he wanted to do, but if he slid into the warm water with her, he wouldn't leave it for hours. And they needed answers about her blood. If she wasn't a five-star female, the first in countless generations, then Vall would eat his training leathers. He'd eat Jay's training leathers.

Finn, Jay and Lyne were waiting for him in the living area. They had all undoubtably had more sleep than he'd managed, propped up against the wall on a stool in Lana's bedroom, but given how he'd spent the time since he woke up to her restless murmurs, he couldn't be sorry.

Finn's nostrils flared as soon as he walked in, Jay and Lyne catching the scent a moment later. He'd showered, but it would take more than that to remove the perfume of Lana's release from his skin, and he hadn't tried all that hard to wash it off anyway. He wanted to smell it on himself, to revel in it, and he wanted others to smell it too, to know she was taken.

Mate.

He thought the word once more. She hadn't objected to the claim as she lay beneath him, lax and sated, though he knew that wasn't quite the same as accepting it. She would, though, in time. She'd already accepted his body in her bed.

"She allowed you to sleep with her?" Finn asked, looking towards the bathing room and Lana.

"No," he denied. He tried not to grin but it was a poor effort.

"You reek of her," Jay growled, his usual good humor dampened by obvious jealousy.

He shrugged. "When she woke this morning, she invited me to her bed."

He'd been pushing, he knew, crowding her, but when he'd smelled her excitement—arousal that hadn't been there when she was sleeping and was for him and him alone—he'd known she would welcome him. And gods, had she made him welcome.

"To pleasure her?" Lyne asked eagerly. "Or did she allow you to mate with her?"

"Can't you tell?" Jay spat out. "Look at his face. He hasn't looked so satisfied since he beat Finn to take Alpha position within the pack."

"He beat you too," Finn grumbled.

"Soundly," Jay agreed. He turned his attention back to Vall. "What was it like? She's not Triniun, is she like our females?"

"Better," Vall replied. "She's sensitive *everywhere*."

Someone groaned quietly.

"And she took you?" Lyne asked. "All of you? She's small."

"It's a tight fit," Vall said, smiling in remembrance, "but gloriously so."

Finn blew out a long breath, no doubt imagining it. He'd be itching to find out for himself. It made everything in Vall roar to contemplate it, but that was how they worked. The pack, not just one male, mated the female. Still, he had no intention of pushing her into Finn's arms. If she wanted to come back to Vall for seconds instead, he wouldn't question it.

"I want to take her to see Danin and Bern," he said, changing the subject. "We need to understand her blood, what it's doing."

"You think it's unsafe?" Finn asked.

"I don't care if it is," Jay butted in. "I don't care if it's poison, I want more of it."

"I would swear on my life it isn't poison," Vall said. "But it's like nothing I've ever tasted before. I think we need to know more."

"You trust them?" Finn said, his glance back to searching the hallway for Lana. "If she is a five-star female, every Warrior in Trinia is going to want to try and snatch her out of our hands."

"Let them try," Lyne snarled, surprising Vall. Lyne was usually the most laid back of the pack. He agreed with him, though. He'd tear apart any other Warrior who dared to challenge for their mate.

"I trust them," he said, his voice rough with restrained aggression, the dragon inside him pushing to be released to protect their female. "And anyone who tries to come for her will die."

Danin and Bern lived in an isolated villa out on the plains. It was hard to get to, deliberately off the beaten track. There were no roads and nothing to point towards it. If Vall hadn't had the exact coordinates to plug into the hover vehicle, he'd never had found it and he'd been there at least a dozen times before. He knew when he saw the small grouping of trees, incongruous amid the endless sand and rock, that they were getting close. The Thinkers had found a tiny oasis in the arid tundra, a natural well that fed a small cluster of flowers and fauna along with their house.

They'd created a laboratory in an underground level beneath the unassuming one-story structure, painted a sand color to blend in with the world around it, so that they could work without having to leave their small slice of Utopia. However, as far as Vall knew, they spent almost all of their time down in the basement with their experiments and their research rather than enjoying the home they had created. Their work was their life.

Decelerating the hover vehicle as they approached, he looked back to where Lana was seated, surrounded by the rest of the pack. Jay had taken the seat opposite her, perched on the edge so his knees were a hairsbreadth from resting against hers. He was talking animatedly, the words hard to discern over the noise of the engine, but whatever it was, Lana was smiling, a slight blush gracing her cheeks. Vall snorted. Jay was likely trying to charm her, encourage her to skip past Finn in the pecking order and take him to her bed next. If the way Finn was glowering at him was any indication, he knew it, too.

He didn't like it either, had every intention of being there to guide the way any — damn it, every — time Lana allowed another member of the pack to touch her and bring her pleasure.

"We're here," he said unnecessarily, killing the engine and drawing Lana's attention back to him. She glanced over at the house, no doubt seeing the security cameras and iron railings covering every window. Danin and Bern liked their privacy, and they didn't like to be interrupted.

They would today, though, when they realized what Vall had brought them.

"Here, Lana," Jay said, getting to his feet and offering his hand. "Let me help you down."

Somewhere in between Lana shifting from seated to standing, though, Jay ended up sprawled back down on his seat and Finn was there instead, taking Lana's elbow and then wrapping his hands around her waist as he lifted her down.

Jay snarled, would have sprung from the hover vehicle, claws extended, if Vall hadn't hauled him back by the collar.

"Calm," he told him, the dominance in his tone and the strength of his grip reining Jay in when the Warrior would have shrugged off his hold and flown at Finn once more. "You'll get your chance, but if you try to subvert the pecking order, Finn will react and I won't stop it." He paused, making sure Jay was listening. "You remember how easily he beat you to take his place as my Second?"

That was cruel, Vall knew it even as he said it, the defeat still a thorn in Jay's pride, but it had the reaction Vall was hoping for. Jay's body lost its rigid tension, his claws sliding back in.

"Besides," Vall said, letting go now that the threat of violence had passed, "how would you feel if you accidentally hurt Lana?"

"I would never —" Jay protested.

"Not on purpose," Vall agreed. "But you might well frighten her enough that she skips right over you."

That got to Jay as nothing else had, not even the force of Vall's alpha dominance. He nodded, gaze going to their mate, who watching them from beside Finn and Lyne, confusion creating a tiny wrinkle between the lines of hair above her eyes. Eyebrows, she'd told Vall when he'd asked her, running a finger along the delicate arches.

"We thought it best to wait for you to knock," Finn commented dryly as Vall and Jay hopped down from the hover vehicle. He inclined his head toward the small screen embedded into the wall beside the front entryway. The door itself was slightly recessed, a crackling electric field barring the way. "I forgot how friendly they were," he added sarcastically."

Vall grinned and approached the screen, his handprint registering when he pressed lightly down onto it. The two Thinkers wouldn't even be notified unless someone whose prints had been registered and approved touched the screen. Strangers would just be left out in the heat to wait until they gave up and went home.

It took a short while, but eventually Danin's face appeared on the screen. He looked tired, his pupils thin lines and his skin dull and dry.

"What?" he asked, peering out at Vall. "In fact, you know what? Never mind what it is. I'm busy, go away."

Expecting this reaction, Vall pulled out the object he'd snagged before leaving the den and holding it up to the screen for Danin to see before he cut them off, which he was clearly about to do.

Danin paused, then squinted and shifted closer to the camera.

"What's that?"

"A weapon."

Danin snorted. "A child could make that. It's not much of a weapon." He was intrigued though. He knew Vall. "Where did you get it?"

"I took it off a saber," Vall said casually.

Danin stared at him for a long hard moment, then switched off the screen. A few seconds later, the forcefield keeping visitors from approaching the front door winked out of existence.

Danin was already there, peering out from around the thick metal barrier.

"Give it to me!" he demanded, holding out his hand.

Vall yielded the weapon willingly enough, sliding an arm around Lana's waist and leading her inside. Danin stepped back enough to let them in, but his attention was fixed on the thing in his hands.

"Metalwork," he said. "They've really progressed to metalwork. I mean, it's a crude start, but it means they've figured out the process. We haven't made metal like this in a millennia, so they must have figured it out on their own." He paused and glanced up distractedly. "Did you speak to the saber you took it from?"

They might have dedicated their lives to researching the Triniun blood problem, but the evolution of the sabers was their hobby, and they were as serious about it as everything else they did.

"He wasn't feeling very talkative." Vall deadpanned.

"You killed him?" Danin frowned.

"That is what I'm paid to do," Vall reminded him.

Danin rolled his eyes and shook his head, muttering to himself as he led them through the house and then downstairs, to the laboratory, shutting off various security systems as he went. If anyone, even a Warrior as experienced as Vall, tried to access this place without Danin and Bern's say so, they'd quickly find themselves oozing across the floor, their bodies sliced up into countless pieces. The pair might not have the build or muscles of Warriors, but they more than made up for that with their minds.

When they entered the laboratory proper, Danin went straight to where Bern was examining something under a microscope, tapping him on the shoulder and handing him the knife wordlessly. Their eyes told Vall they were carrying on the conversation, though — using the Thinkers' telepathic abilities. They'd tried it on Vall once, pushing the words into his head. He'd gotten a brief flash of what they were trying to say, but also a blinding headache.

"You killed it?" Bern asked, frowning unhappily.

"Afraid so."

He sighed heavily, then took in the entourage violating the sanctuary of the laboratory, particularly Lana. Vall tightened his arm around her waist protectively, though this was exactly why they'd come.

"Lana," he said. "This is Danin and his partner, Bern."

"An unmarked female?" Bern asked. Then he shook his head, shifting off his stool. "No, she's not Triniun."

Vall tried not to grin. They'd managed to gain admittance

and now had piqued Bern's interest. The Thinkers would definitely help them now.

"She's not," he agreed. "Her planet is a place called Earth. She came through the transporter by accident and an Administrator put her into the challenges as a tribute."

"He couldn't send her back?" Danin asked, surprised.

"Apparently not."

"I died," Lana said suddenly. She spoke quietly, but the words echoed around the room.

"What?" Vall pressed, tugging her round so he could pull her into his arms properly.

"I died," she repeated, that little line between her eyebrows back again, a sign of her unhappiness. "I was in a car crash. I mean, Rin said he couldn't send me back anyway because he didn't know where to send me, but I don't know that he could have even if he'd wanted to."

"Rin?" Bern asked quietly.

"The Administrator," Vall told him, his gaze fixed on his little mate. She was upset, her shoulders hunching and her eyes glistening. "You never told me this."

She gave a small shrug. "There hasn't been much of an opportunity." She pulled in a deep breath. "I told you I wasn't supposed to be there, you never asked why."

"I am . . .sorry, Lana."

Shame rolled through Vall. She was right, he hadn't asked. He'd been too blinded by the euphoric taste of her blood, the dragon demanding he take her and run. A tiny part of him was relieved, though. He didn't want her to even think about leaving him. Them. Not ever. He pulled her to him, gripped by strong emotion, a hand cupping the back of her head and turned back to Danin and Bern.

"She hasn't been tested."

"That's why you're here?" Danin asked, scrunching up his face in displeasure. "To ask us to test a random female? There are centers for that. Do you know how important our work is? We're—"

The guttural snarl that came from Vall's chest choked the words in Danin's throat, his eyes widening as he backed toward his partner.

""I need you to test her," Vall told him, voice little more than a growl, "because there is something special about her. Her blood, it's . . .it wakens my dragon."

It took a moment for that to sink in with the two Thinkers, but when it did, they turned and gaped at Lana.

CHAPTER TEN

I didn't know what it was about Vall's words that made the men—Thinkers, Vall had told me they were called—gasp, but it threw them into motion. Danin grabbed up a tablet, his fingers flying across the screen, as the other one—Bern?— picked up a small piece of equipment that looked a bit like a gun, the key element of which, at least to my mind, was the needle glinting on the end.

I stepped back instinctively—I'd never liked injections and I *really* didn't like the idea of letting two strange aliens jab at me—but Vall held me fast.

"It's a simple blood draw," he soothed. "It won't hurt."

I very much doubted that, but I stood still and let the Thinker approach me. He gave me what I gathered was supposed to be a reassuring smile, but the avarice in his eyes killed the effect. He took my wrist and turned it, exposing my inner arm to his little machine. I winced, my bicep tensing involuntarily, but between Vall's arms around me and Bern's firm grip on my wrist, I didn't have anywhere to go. There was a sharp scratch and a small sting. It lasted only a heartbeat before Bern retracted the device and let me go. I yanked my arm back, holding it protectively up against my chest and glaring at him even though it hadn't really hurt.

"You should test me also," Vall volunteered. "I feel . . .changed."

I felt a little better when Bern came back, pushing the needle against Vall's arm—Danin already busy shoving my sample into another machine—especially when I saw how much harder he had to press against Vall's inner arm to pierce his tougher skin. I reached out and ran my fingers along the spot, feeling the difference between us. His arm was completely hairless, but the skin was tougher, almost amphibian in texture, though it was much more supple, the muscle in his forearm twitching in response to my touch.

Vall's gaze was hot on mine, just that small touch rousing something in him. I wasn't going to pretend not to like that. He opened his mouth to speak, but Danin made a shocked little noise, distracting us both.

"What?" Vall asked, crossing the room to peer over Danin's shoulder and taking me with him. "What is it?"

Danin was typing into his tablet again, symbols flying across the screen.

"I ran her blood through the generic test first," he said, then he gave a little grunt that I think was supposed to pass for humor. "She should not be unmarked."

"She's a five-star female?" Vall asked. "I knew it!"

"No," Danin mumbled distractedly.

"No?" Vall looked a little disappointed. "Four then? She cannot be less!" he exclaimed when Danin gave a little shake of his head.

"She is not."

"Six?" Vall sounded astounded. "I've never heard of a six-star female, not even in our history."

"Not six," Danin corrected. "Seven."

Utter silence descended on the laboratory, broken only by the small sounds of Bern feeding Vall's sample into a different machine, this one a strange circular shape, which started spinning at speed as soon as the sample tube was clicked into place.

"Seven stars?" Finn gasped, approaching us. "Is that even possible?"

"Apparently so," Danin replied sardonically.

"Seven stars," I heard Lyne mutter behind me. "Gods."

"Is that good or bad?" I asked, looking from face to face.

"It is unheard of," Danin supplied, not very helpfully. I turned to Vall, who was recovering enough from his shock to unfurl a grin.

"It is wondrous," he assured me. He turned to Danin. "You are sure?"

The Thinker didn't bother to reply, just made a scornful noise because Vall questioned his word. "I'll just create an entry for her in the register, then I can do her markings."

"Stop!" Vall's command was accompanied by a hand landing hard on Danin's shoulder. The Thinker froze, the gaze he turned toward Vall cautious. "Don't enter her into the register."

"I have to," Danin said slowly. "It's the law."

"I don't give a fuck about the law. You put that entry in there, you put a beacon on her."

"And your answer is what? To hide her away? Pretend she doesn't exist? I think other Warriors may start asking hard questions if you are right and she has awakened your dragon. You don't think they might wonder why there are fully formed beasts soaring in the sky after a millennia of nothing but clouds?"

I didn't think the Danin's tone was particularly wise given the furious look on Vall's face. He didn't flinch, though I could practically hear the bones crunch in his shoulder as Vall tightened his grip.

"You will not be able to hide this," he continued softly. "If you try to, they may use it as grounds to take her away from you when it eventually comes out."

"I will let no one take her from me," Vall growled.

"You and your pack against every Warrior in Trinia? You'd die, and either she'd die, too, in the furor, or she'd be left vulnerable and unprotected afterwards."

I drew in a sharp breath, certain Vall was going to explode — and he wasn't the only one; I could hear a low growl coming from one of the rest of the pack in the background — but after clenching his jaw hard for a long, tension-filled moment, Vall deliberately loosened his grip and let Danin go.

"I can bury the entry," the Thinker offered. "Make it so that it doesn't flag unless someone is looking for her specifically."

"Thank you," Vall replied through gritted teeth.

Danin nodded and tapped away for a few moments, then he stood and reached up high to pull a machine down from a shelf above his head. It was covered in a light coating of dust which he blew on it before pressing a button to test it.

"It's not calibrated to create seven stars," he said, looking down at it. "But I can work around it."

I leaned back into Vall, very unsure about this. The thing in Danin's hand looked like nothing so much as a tattoo gun, and he was going to put it to my face? Tattoo the skin just beneath my eye? What if his hand slipped? What if he sneezed and the thing jumped, needles stabbing into my eyeball?

"Lana," Vall murmured, shifting so that he was slightly behind me, his arms around my waist and his head down so that his mouth was by my ear. "You're trembling."

"How does it work?" I asked nervously. "What if he misses and damages my eye?"

"I won't," Danin replied, offended.

Right.

"Does it hurt?"

"Babies go through this," he said, the frown wrinkling his eyebrow-less forehead telling me he thought I was being childish. Well, babies dealt with circumcision too, but full-grown men weren't exactly lining up to have the procedure done, were they?

"It will not hurt," Vall crooned. He glanced up to Danin. "If it does, I will rip his arms off."

I barked a laugh at that, but I was the only one. As Danin approached me, Finn came up behind him, arms folded to emphasis his large biceps and a scowl on his face that warned of violence if I so much as made a pained little whimper. Danin ignored him, pretending to be unaffected, but I started to worry that they'd intimidate him into messing up. I didn't want my stars, but if I had to have them, I didn't want them blurred and wonky, either.

I tried to calm myself, releasing the tension in my shoulders, determined not to make a sound even if it hurt. Danin pressed the machine to the left side my face, beneath my eye just where my cheekbone met my nose and I felt it vibrate. There was no sharp pinch of a needle, but my skin felt hot to the point of burning. Slowly, he drew it along toward my ear, leaving a trail of tingling, tight feeling skin. When he let up, moving his hand back a fraction, I exhaled heavily, but he wasn't done.

"Hold still," he warned. "Just a moment longer."

He started at the outside this time, the machine pressed a little lower and he only drew it along a short way before stopping and stepping back entirely.

"Is that it?" I asked. "Is it done?"

Vall practically shoved Danin aside in his hurry to get in front of me. He peered down into my face, hand cupping my jaw.

"Are you all right?" he asked.

"It burned," I admitted. "But it wasn't too bad. How . . .how does it look?"

Danin silently handed Vall his tablet, and when Vall lifted it up in front of me, I could see my face reflected on the screen like a front facing camera. I looked wild, my eyes wide with adrenaline, my skin pale. My left cheek was a vivid pink color, but the stars themselves were black. They were neat, clustered together in a row of five, with two tucked down on a line below. They looked exactly like the stars I'd seen on the other tributes, except that I had seven of them.

"It's not going to matter if her name's on a register if she's walking around with her blood purity on her face, is it?" Jay commented, his gaze concerned as he, too, came to look.

"We can protect her," Vall said. "And Danin is right, we have to do things properly. I will give them no excuse to try and take her from us."

"Maybe I can just stay in the house." I said it as a joke, but a look at Vall's somber expression told me he was seriously considering it.

"What about my blood?" he asked, turning to Bern. "Do you see anything in it?"

Bern had been silent up until this point, busy with whatever he was doing with Vall's sample. He lifted his head up from the microscope he'd been squinting into and gave Vall an exasperated look.

"I've only had it for five minutes. Patience, Warrior. I'll contact you when I know what I'm looking at."

I could see that Vall wanted answers — and he wanted them now — but he settled for a short nod. He glanced back at Danin, who had taken the tablet out of my hands and was fluttering away at the screen with his fingers once more.

"You'll tell no one?" Vall asked, though it was more of a growled demand.

"Who am I going to tell?" Danin asked. "Who even knows you're here? If her blood status is revealed, it will not have come from me. Though you're a fool if you hope to keep it secret for long."

Vall snorted, patting Danin on the shoulder in a friendly gesture that might have been a little more forceful than necessary.

"I'll be waiting to hear from you," he said. "I thank you for your help today."

Neither Bern nor Danin escorted us back up and out. Instead, each door we'd gone through to get down there in the first place closed behind us with a resounding thunk and a buzz that spoke of multiple locks engaging. It was like a nuclear bunker on steroids, I couldn't imagine spending an extended amount of time down there without going crazy from the claustrophobia.

Stepping back out into the sunshine was a breath of fresh air, even if that air was hot, humid and choked with dust. Vall helped me onto the hover vehicle, then sat down and pulled me onto his lap, leaving the piloting to Finn. As the vehicle picked up speed, I turned into him, resting my head on his shoulder. The adrenaline I'd felt in Danin and Bern's laboratory had faded and now I just felt wiped. Vall didn't complain, wrapping his arms around me and nuzzling at my hair. A moment later, I felt his hands begin to rove, running up the length of my thigh and tracing the curve of my waist. When he ran his fingertips featherlight over the side of my breast, I stirred, twitching away from him.

"No?" he asked, in a voice low enough not to carry beyond the two of us. "You enjoy my touch."

I did. Oh, I did, but I was also acutely aware of Jay and Lyne sitting not six feet away and watching us, and also of Finn, whose head kept turning in my direction.

"You're shy," he guessed. "There's no need to be. With Warriors, the whole pack mates the female. To accept one is to accept all of us."

So they did share a woman. I sucked in a gasp, shocked, but I'd be lying if I said I wasn't intrigued by the idea. Drawing back a little bit, I looked over at Jay and Lyne, whose gazes were riveted to the two of us, to Vall's fingers, which had gone back to stroking, brushing up and down against the skin on my side, a hairsbreadth from my breast. I could have shifted my arm and trapped his hand, arrested his movement. For that matter, I could have dislodged him entirely. I didn't.

"That's not how we do things where I'm from," I stammered.

"But you're not there," he argued. "You're here."

He had me there. As Jay caught and held my stare, Vall sucked my earlobe into his mouth, used his tongue to rim the delicate edge of my ear. I felt a pulse start pounding between my legs, my breasts almost hurting with their need to be touched. Slowly, deliberately, I shifted a little on Vall's lap so that my breast grazed his hand, his knuckle trailing over my nipple. It was through my clothes, the knee-length tunic and leggings I was wearing as another hand-me-down, but I felt it like a streak of fire. I made an inarticulate little sound, arching my back in the hopes that he'd do it again.

He did, his other hand cupping the back of my head and ensuring that I didn't look away from where Jay and Lyne were watching me, Jay so far forward on the seat he looked ready to fall off at any moment.

"I smell your excitement, Lana," Vall whispered to me. "I think you like them watching you. Do you want to call them over here, have them go to their knees in front of you? Would you let them play with your pretty breasts?"

He let go of my hair to cup both breasts, lifting them slightly in his hands as if he was offering them to the other two Warriors. When he swiped his thumbs across both my nipples in one firm movement, my whole lower body clenched and I cried out.

"Well?" he murmured. "Should I?"

I was a heartbeat away from saying *yes* when Finn interrupted.

"Vall, we're being hailed." He paused. "It's High Defender Ginn."

Vall ran his fingertips one more time along the underside of my breast, then dropped his hands to my waist. He sighed heavily. "I cannot ignore this," he told me. "Forgive me, Lana."

Taking a firm grip, he lifted me off his lap and deposited me on the seat. His erection tented his trousers when he stood, and he paused to adjust himself with a grimace before moving to where Finn waited at the controls. Curious, I shifted a little closer, straining to catch the conversation. I didn't have to try hard. The High Defender, whoever he was, had a booming voice that travelled easily.

"Ridian," he shouted. "Where the fuck have you been? I've been getting no answer to my hails, don't you have your personal communicator with you?"

"I'm sorry, sir," Vall replied. "I'm out in the plains, there's no signal."

"What the hell are you doing out there?"

Vall looked over to me and I didn't bother to pretend not to be listening in.

"Visiting old friends."

The High Defender took a moment to answer. "Your friends have interesting taste in scenery." The suspicion in his tone was obvious.

"They are unusual individuals," Vall agreed.

"Well, I hope you're nearly back, because I'm heading to your place. I want to talk to you about the saber problem. I've just had an earful from the Sovereign and I'm ready to pass that shafting on to someone else."

"You're coming to the pack den?"

"That's what I said. I'll be there shortly, so get your ass back. Out."

Static hissed out of the speaker before Finn twirled a button and quieted it. "Shit," he muttered, glancing back at me. "Danin was right, Vall. We aren't going to be able to hide her."

"That's as may be," Vall replied, a heavy frown on his face

74

as he, too, contemplated me. "But that doesn't mean we have to wave her in front of people's faces, the High Defender included. Jay, Lyne, when we get back to the den, you take her straight to her bedroom and stay there. We'll leave introductions to our illustrious leader for another day." He turned to Finn. "I want to get there before him."

Giving a grim nod, Finn accelerated hard and the hover vehicle responded, flying across the sands until the landscape around me became nothing more than a blur.

CHAPTER ELEVEN

We arrived before the High Defender, the landing pad in front of the house — that I now knew sat on a ridge in the foothills above the city — still empty when Finn guided the hover vehicle in to land. It was a close-run thing, though. As soon as Finn cut the engine, I became aware of the drone of another vehicle, getting steadily louder.

"Take her inside," Vall commanded.

Jay took the instruction literally, sweeping me off my feet and jumping lightly down from the vehicle with me in his arms. He grinned at the small, undignified squeak I let out, hurrying me through the house until we reached the large bedroom that had been given to me. At first I thought he was just going to throw me down onto the bed. A tiny part of me was actually hoping that he might — and follow me down — but he placed me gently back on my feet beside it instead. Lyne had followed us into the house, but veered off somewhere between the door and my bedroom. It was just me and Jay, who was giving me a look I imagined a tiger might give a bunny rabbit, right before he ate it.

"How long do you think we're going to have to stay in this room?" I asked.

Jay shrugged, smiling impishly. "However long it takes. Hopefully a long time."

I looked around the room. Aside from a low stool and empty table, a chest filled with the clothes I'd been pilfering, there was literally nothing in the room but the bed. There wasn't even a balcony to go out on and admire the view.

"What are we going to do?"

Stupid question. Jay's response was a long, slow grin. I looked away from him, flustered, but then my gaze landed on the bed and all I could imagine was the two of us on there, tangled up in the sheets.

"What are you thinking about?" he murmured, eyes half closing to narrow slits. He drew in a deep breath and I remembered how good their sense of smell was.

"Food," I blurted. "I'm hungry."

The smile he gave me was absolutely lethal. "Me too."

Was there anything the man couldn't turn into sex?

I wasn't used to flirty men, not like this. Handsome charmers tended to focus their attention on other women—younger ones, with prettier faces and perkier tits. I wasn't ugly or some sort of wallflower, but I was woefully unprepared for Jay's teasing sexuality.

I looked to the door, thinking to escape before I burst into flames, the High Defender be damned, but Lyne appeared there, blocking the way.

"You're hungry?" he asked. In his hands he had a large tray full of food.

"Yes, please!" I seized on the idea like a lifeline, rushing over to Lyne and hovering as he placed the tray down on the table. There were little bowls of something that looked a bit like chili or stew and a big fruit platter piled high with different berries and sliced fruits. Three small tumblers filled with dark liquid took up the rest of the space on the tray.

There was only one stool, so I sat while Jay and Lyne towered above me as we ate the stew. It was a little spicey for my taste, and I found myself cooling my mouth down with the drink, which was some sort of fruit juice. I didn't realize until I'd finished my stew and was sipping the rest of my drink, my tongue losing the sting of the spice, that there was a strong alcoholic kick. Oops.

Between the food and the boozy juice, I was feeling pleasantly warm, listening to Jay and Lyne's low conversation about what the High Defender might want. A personal visit was apparently an unusual occurrence, and from the little glimpse Lyne had got when he'd passed by the living area on his way back from the kitchen, the High Defender hadn't looked happy.

"We'll find out," Jay eventually said with a shrug. He glanced down at me and saw I was watching the two of them with slightly glassy eyes. A sly smile split his face and he picked up the platter the fruit was laid out on. "Are you ready for dessert?" he asked me.

I was beginning to think more food in my stomach might be a good way to counteract the alcohol, so I nodded, reaching for a slice of something that looked like pear.

"Nuh uh." Jay snagged my wrist, holding it and lifting the platter out of my reach at the same time. "That isn't how this works. If you want a treat, you have to come over here and get it."

He reversed until the back of his legs hit the bed, then he sprawled across it, lifting up on his side, the platter of fruit on the covers just in front of him. There was a challenge in his eyes as he patted a spot on the other side of the plate, inviting me to join him. I hesitated, but then some hitherto dormant reckless streak woke up inside me and whispered that I should do it. Ignoring all the much louder, much more sensible voices saying this was a bad idea, I got up and strolled over to him in as seductive a walk as I was capable of. The bed was the perfect height for him, but high for me. I lifted a knee up and was about to give a little jump to get myself up there — which would have been a lot less sexy — when hands gripped me from behind and lifted me up enough that I could transfer my weight onto the mattress and start crawling over toward Jay.

"Good girl," he called softly.

I lay down opposite him and felt an immediate warmth at my back as Lyne stretched out behind me. The sensible voices in my head squeaked in alarm, but the naughty little dare-devil hissed that I should stay right there. Astonished at my own brazenness, I wriggled to get more comfortable, cozying back further in Lyne as I did so. He went still for an instant, that I felt a gentle hand start stroking through my unruly tresses, tugging on them lightly and setting off tiny tingles across my scalp. I closed my eyes briefly, enjoying the sensation — I *loved* people playing with my hair — then I reached for a piece of fruit.

Jay foiled me again, this time slapping at my hand.

He tutted at me, shaking his head like he was disappointed, then lifted the bit of fruit I'd been going for.

"*This* is how we eat the fruit," he said, bringing it up to my lips.

I thought about clamping my lips shut, pointing out that I could eat my own food, thank you very much, but I'd let Vall feed me dinner just the night before. I opened my mouth, expecting Jay to slip it in, but he painted my lips with it instead, the fruit still in his fingers when he leaned forward and licked off the juice.

"I thought this was my dessert," I said breathlessly when he pulled back.

"It's called sharing," he murmured.

Sharing indeed. Lyne was still running his fingers through my hair, though he'd pulled it off my shoulder, exposing the skin. He ran his nose up the curve, sniffing deeply, then followed the same track again, this time with tiny kisses.

My lips parted on a gasp and Jay fed me the slice of fruit. "Eat," he coaxed.

It didn't taste like pear. It tasted like wickedness and indulgence, and I gazed at Jay, eager for more.

He took a berry next. He offered it to me, letting me crane my neck to reach for it, but then he pulled back and tossed it into his own mouth.

"Mmmm," he said, winking at me.

Caught up in the moment, forgetting I was sensible Lana Murray who didn't get entangled in these sorts of situations, I pouted. "Aren't we sharing?"

Jay swallowed the mouthful of fruit then grinned at me. "We are."

He leaned forward and kissed me, a real kiss this time, his mouth parting mine and his tongue sliding inside. He tasted like the fruit he'd just eaten, and I licked at him, drinking in the flavor. When I pulled back, Lyne had a grip on the hair he'd been stroking, and he tilted my head so that he could kiss me, too. He'd obviously stolen some fruit while I wasn't looking, and I savored the clean, tart taste. I would have expected Lyne's kiss to be softer than Jay's, gentler, but instead it was harder, more demanding, his hand in my hair refusing to let me move an inch. By the time he finally lifted up and gave me space to breath, I was gasping.

"Are you all right?" Jay asked, pulling my attention back to him. "You're looking very flushed. Maybe you're too warm." He flicked his gaze up to Lyne. "We don't want her to overheat."

"What?" I asked, blinking stupidly. "No, I'm—"

Before I had time to finish the sentence, Lyne moved to kneel on the bed. He tilted my shoulders up to rest on his thighs, his hands reaching down and grasping the hem of my tunic top. He glided it up and off, baring me from the waist. I wasn't wearing a bra because I hadn't been able to find anything like that in the chest of clothes and I'd been too embarrassed to ask. As I lay before Jay and sprawled across Lyne, both of their gazes raking over my half naked body, I regretted that cowardice. Mostly.

"Beautiful," Lyne murmured and my hands, which had been slowly edging upward to cover myself, stilled.

"Hold onto her, Lyne," Jay said, reaching for a dark purple fruit the shape of a chili pepper. He nipped the end off with his teeth. "I don't want her wriggling around while I'm working."

Lyne reached down and snagged both of my hands, lifting them up and over my head until they were resting against his hips. I tugged a little, but he tightened his grip infinitesimally, holding me there.

Jay, meanwhile, had pushed the rest of the platter to the side and shifted position on the bed until he was resting between my legs, elbows leaning on the mattress on either side of my middle.

"Where to start?" he wondered.

Reaching up, he drew the bleeding end of the fruit across one collar bone, circled the hollow of my throat, and then continuing down the other. It tickled, the leeching juices leaving a wet trail that tingled slightly in the cool air of the room. As I watched, he went back to the center and drew a line down, right between my breasts all the way down to my belly button. This time I could see the light purple residue it was leaving on my skin.

"We can't leave out these beautiful breasts," Jay told me, shifting his focus there. He drew lightly around the undersides and then circled the outer edges of the areola of my left breast. He paused, looking up at me to make sure I was watching. When he saw that he had my undivided attention he smiled, circling inward in tiny increments, drawing the moment out until at last he ran it over the tip of my nipple.

I flinched, squirming against his weight on my pelvis, and that earned me another grin. "Lick it off," I demanded.

"Listen to her," he said conversationally to Lyne. "Making demands." He shook his head at me. "I'm not finished painting." To punctuate his point, he blew on my wetted nipple, making it tighten almost to the point of pain.

I cried out, pulling against Lyne's hold, needy and frustrated, but they both just laughed.

"You're supposed to be enjoying this," Jay told me.

"I would," I snapped back, "if you'd just hurry up."

That earned me another chuckle and a head shake, Jay returning to paint those lazy circles around my right breast. If anything, he drew it out even longer this time, his dark eyes watching me, daring to complain. I kept my mouth shut, watching him greedily, my breath speeding up as he reached the center.

This time he didn't make me suffer. As soon as the fruit had flicked off the end of my nipple, he was there with his mouth, latching on hard, drawing the whole thing into his mouth and sucking, his tongue rubbing my aching tip against the roof of his mouth.

It was bliss. I pressed my head back into Lyne, trying to lift my hips to grind into Jay, though I couldn't get any purchase.

"What about her other side?" Lyne asked, amused, when Jay lifted his head, mouth shiny and wet.

"I'm leaving that for you," Jay told him.

"No," I gasped, struggling to sit up. This time Lyne let me. "It's my turn."

Surprise flickered across Jay's face for a moment, then he surrendered, dropping the fruit back onto the platter with a wet plopping sound and lying back against my pillows.

"I am yours to torture," he offered.

Good. Because I intended to.

Going up on my knees between his leather-clad thighs, I ran my hands over his bare chest. Shirts were apparently not part of the Warrior dress code, though he did have cuffs tied tightly around both forearms and decorative bands around his impressive biceps.

"This is quite the canvas," I said, my heart pounding at my own daring. "But it isn't where I want to paint."

I dropped my hands down to his trousers and started working at the clasp. It wasn't like any belt buckle I'd seen before, but I fumbled at it and after a moment it sprang free. I tried to ease his trousers over his hips, but they were tight-fitting and after a moment Jay rolled to the side slightly so he could quickly divest himself of them.

"Eager," I commented, when he twisted back into position.

"You have no idea," he said.

Smug, I dropped my gaze and got a good look at his cock for the first time. With Vall, I hadn't even got my hands on it, it had simply been in me, making stars explode behind my eyes. Now I was going to get to play. I liked cocks, as a rule. I liked the heat in my hands, the way they stood up when engorged, like they were reaching for me. Jay's cock was beautiful. It was long and thick and I didn't know if they circumcised men here, but there was no foreskin to hide the glistening tip from my view. A vein traced the length down to his balls, which were full and hairless.

I ignored the chili-shaped fruit—just in case it *was* spicy—and picked up a berry. Biting it in half, I chewed and swallowed one half while pretending to study his lower body.

"Hmmm," I murmured. "Where to start? Maybe here?" I outlined the curve of his balls with the fruit, circling each and then running the berry up the middle until I reached the base of his shaft. I couldn't see the pale pink of the fruit's flesh against his darker skin, but it glistened wetly as I left a trail that made the delicate sac wrinkle and pucker as his balls tightened. "Or here?" I ran all the way up his length in one smooth movement, lifting the fruit away before I reached the tip, which bobbled slightly in impatience.

"She's a tease," Lyne said from over my shoulder.

"Turnabout is fair play," I commented.

"I'm enjoying it," Jay told me, his eyes gleaming in narrow slits. If he could, I think he'd have been purring. "Though I warn you not to tease Lyne like this. He gets a little wound up."

"You're giving away all my secrets," Lyne complained, making me shiver as he began stroking lightly up my back with the tips of his claws.

"I'll keep that in mind," I said to Jay, touching the tip of his cock with the berry with the lightest contact I could manage. I started at the slit and worked my way outward, circling and circling. Jay's eyes closed entirely and he might have been asleep if it hadn't been for his hands, clenched into tight fists and the rigid tension outlining every muscle in his upper body. It was an incredible sight, one that made me feel horny and gloriously sexy and powerful all at the same time.

Done with torturing both of us, I ate the rest of the berry and leaned forward. I started at his balls, swiping at the drying juices with long licks of my tongue, then running the tip all the way up to his head. By the time I'd reached the top, his hand was in my hair, urging me to open my mouth and engulf him. There was no point denying us what we both wanted, so I stretched my mouth wide and took him in, feeling him out with my tongue and searching for all the remnants of the berry juice.

I started a steady rhythm, pulsing up and down, sucking at the head and taking as much as I could of his shaft into my mouth, using my hand to grip the long inches that I couldn't. My motions stuttered when I felt Lyne tugging at my trousers, pulling them down and off, but Jay's hand urged me to continue, guiding me into the speed he wanted.

I felt Lyne's hands urge me to widen my stance then the tickle of his hair, freed from its ponytail, on my inner thighs a moment before a hot tongue was licking at my slit and questing for entrance. I pulled back, shocked and stared at Jay, who was watching me with hooded eyes while another man licked my pussy. I'd never done anything like this before.

"It's all right," he soothed. "Just relax and enjoy it."

I hesitated a moment longer, biting my lip as Lyne pushed deeper with his tongue, sliding an inch inside me, then I tried to do as Jay said, dropping down and concentrating on licking and sucking on Jay's cock. When Lyne found my clit, flicking at it firmly, I moaned, my body convulsing, teeth scraping lightly as I pulled back. Jay stopped me from lifting up entirely, groaning, "Do that again, Lyne. Whatever you just did. Fuck."

He pushed me back down, a bit deeper, a bit more forceful, and I responded by unveiling my teeth, letting them rake against the underside of his shaft. I'd never have done this with any of my past lovers, but the Warriors' skin was a little thicker than a normal man's, and judging by the way Jay had finally lost hold of his controlled stillness, it felt good.

Now that Lyne had discovered my clit, he seemed determined to play with it, flicking at it from every angle before putting his whole mouth around it and sucking. That made me buck, my hips trying to lift up and grind down at the same time, and Lyne had to wrap his arms around me to hold me in place, a sharp nip from his teeth on my inner thigh coming along with a guttural *Hold still.*

Holding still was impossible, though, especially when Jay reached down and pinched my nipples, saying, "Concentrate." It was like an assault on all sides, Lyne's tongue on my clit, a finger teasing my entrance, Jay leaving a hand on one breast to cup and squeeze and roll and pinch while the other one went to my head and pushed me deeper, forced me to move faster. I couldn't breathe, I couldn't move and I—

The orgasm hit me from out of nowhere. Trapped between the two unyielding males, it didn't roll through me so much as implode and then burst outward once more. I wasn't aware of Jay's own release until his seed was overflowing my mouth. Mindless, I tried to lick and swallow what I could, but I was pulled up and off as Lyne hissed, "Lana." His cock was suddenly in my face, his hand gripping the shaft, trousers torn open and ripped down low onto his hips. I opened wide, thinking he wanted me to take him in my mouth as well, but he was already coming, pearly white streams erupting from his tip and landing on my mouth and chin, dropping down to splatter on my breasts.

"Fuck," he grunted. "Fuck."

He guided me forward and rubbed the head on my mouth, smearing his ejaculate across my lips until I opened them and let him paint it on my tongue.

He was panting and so was I, endorphins fizzing in my blood stream. He pulled back and rested his weight on his heels, those magic fingers stroking my slightly sweaty hair again. The look in his eyes was almost frighteningly intense, but it was also full of adoration.

"See," Jay murmured, arms coming around me from behind to hug me to his chest. "That's how you eat dessert."

Chapter Twelve

The High Defender did not normally do house calls. That alone told Vall the shit had seriously hit the fan. He stood to attention on the landing platform, Finn by his side, and waited as High Defender Ginn climbed out of his vehicle. He'd travelled with an entourage of three Warriors—Tan, Malin and Heo—who were the remnants of an unusually large pack of seven that had been torn apart during the war with Xanan more than a decade ago. Becoming personal guard to the High Defender had given them a new lease of life, and normally the brothers were full of smiles and jokes. Today, even their faces were grim, Heo's mouth an unhappy line as he stood ready to help Ginn down.

The older man waved his assistance away, a sharp retort causing the Warrior to step back and drop his head. He stayed by the vehicle when Ginn, Malin and Tan approached Vall.

"Sir." Vall gave a sharp, respectful salute.

"Knock it off with that shit, will you, Ridian? My balls are cooking. Let's get inside where it's cooler."

"As you wish, sir." Vall led the group inside to the open living area, gaze raking the space to make sure Jay and Lyne had done their job and gotten Lana to the privacy of her bedroom. There was no sign of their mate, though Vall caught the shadow of Lyne ghosting past the doorway from the direction of the kitchen, a tray in his hand. He nodded approvingly at his pack member. Food would hopefully keep Lana occupied until after the High Defender was gone.

Malin and Tao took up positions in discreet corners of the

room while Ginn levered himself slowly down onto the sofa. Finn, too, stayed standing, taking up a post by the silent fireplace, close enough to hear what was happening and engage, if necessary, but leaving the lead role to Vall, who took a spot on the other side of the L-shaped sofa from Ginn. Sometimes it was good to be Alpha, other times, like this, when he suspected he was going to get a serious dressing-down, it was a pain in the ass.

"I've just come from the Sovereign's palace," the High Defender said. "He is . . .unhappy."

Judging by the expression on Ginn's face, Vall guessed the Sovereign was a long way from just unhappy.

"What's the reason this time?" he asked.

Ginn gave him a warning look, though Vall knew from past conversations that the High Defender agreed with him. The Sovereign ruled the planet and all the surrounding occupied moons, but he did so with a tight-knit group of Thinkers and Administrators who did most of the actual work. Danin and Bern had been two of the Sovereign's highest advisors at one point before they got tired of his dramatics. The man was useless as leaders went, but he'd inherited the title along with an army that was the largest in Trinia's history — despite their current peaceful relationships with nearby planets — along with a small collection of assassins. He used those ruthlessly against anyone stupid enough to speak out against him, so challenges to his right to rule were few and far between.

"He has a summer house in the western valleys," Ginn continued.

Vall nodded. He'd been there once before, called in to provide additional security when the Sovereign had thrown an enormous party to celebrate his fiftieth year of rule. What the Sovereign called a summer house was a mansion in most people's eyes, and it sat empty for most of the year. It had been a bastard to secure, too, with windows everywhere to make the most of the views — and provide anyone with nefarious intentions an easy point of access.

"Crews were sent there last week to prepare the place for the Sovereign to convalesce after a busy time in the capital and they discovered the summer house had been vandalized."

"Vandalized?" Vall asked. "By citizens?"

Ginn set his jaw. "I believe the destruction took the form of claws down the curtains and pissing on the furniture."

"Sabers," Vall said, finally understanding. He frowned. "I've never heard of nests in that region."

"There aren't any."

"You think they're migrating?" He stared at the High Defender, saw the worry in his hard gaze.

"No," he said. "That's not it."

Understanding hit him along with a healthy dose of astonishment. "You think they travelled there on purpose? That it was targeted?"

Ginn nodded slowly.

"But to do that, they'd have to know he was the Sovereign. They'd have to understand that he had multiple residences, know that the summer house belongs to him. They'd have to plan to hit it when the place was empty." Which, admittedly, was most of the time. Still . . ."That's a lot of thinking for sabers. They aren't that intelligent. They don't strategize like that."

"They *didn't*," Ginn replied, his words heavy with meaning. "I think they're evolving more quickly than we realized. Of course, they have us to look to as examples."

Vall snorted. "I hope they don't look too closely. We're not as civilized as we like to pretend." He thought about the small metal knife he'd taken from the body of the saber in the forest, the one Danin had been so interested in. A stubby knife was a long way from organized fucking thinking, though. "You're sure?"

"No, I'm not sure. I suspect." Ginn leaned forward slightly, and Vall had a feeling they were finally coming to the crux of it. "I need you to find out one way or the other. Well, first of all I need you to kill the damned sabers who sprayed all over the Sovereign's fancy fainting couch and tore up his favorite curtains."

"Those exact sabers?" Vall asked, raising his eyes. "How the hell am I supposed to do that? They'll be long gone and, I don't know if you've noticed, High Defender, but even if you've got security footage, they all look the same."

"Just find me some sabers I can skin and hand to the Sovereign, all right?" he snapped back.

Vall rolled his eyes, but nodded. "I can manage that."

"Good. Thank you." Sarcasm dripped from his tone. "But once you've done that, I need to know if this is just a random incident, or if they really are beginning to think and plan like, well, like . . ."

"People?" Vall suggested softly.

"That's the rub, isn't it," Ginn replied darkly. "If they are people, what the fuck are we doing?"

Vall nodded somberly. The High Defender's visit hadn't come with the reaming he expected, but it was worse for that. If Ginn's suspicions were right and the sabers were evolving into something with more thought, more reasoning than the pests — the animals — they'd always been taken for, then what Vall and his pack had been doing, what all the Warriors had been doing recently, was nothing less than murder.

"Where's your new thrall?" Ginn asked suddenly, changing the subject entirely. "I heard you claimed one in the challenges."

The predator inside Vall rose to deadly alertness, sensing a threat, though he tried not to show it on his face.

"I did," he said slowly. "She is here, but she's shy. It's an adjustment for her. I believe she would prefer not to be introduced, if you would forgive the rudeness."

Ginn nodded, but it was easily to see the frustrated curiosity in his gaze. His turned his eyes to look at the hallway leading to the rest of the den, as if she might suddenly appear.

"What's her name?" he asked.

"Lana."

The High Defender's brow raised a fraction. "Unusual. Which region is she from?"

Was he being herded? Vall eyed Ginn suspiciously. It was a direct question, though, and he couldn't lie to the High Defender. He also didn't want to lie to the man he called a friend.

"She's not from Trinia," he said. "She came to the challenges from outside the sector."

Ginn wanted to ask more, Vall could tell that, but the old man wasn't stupid. Vall was practically radiating reluctance, and Finn, by the fireplace, was twitching with agitation.

"Well, I look forward to meeting her when she's become more acclimatized," he said diplomatically. He wasn't quite done, though. "Has she been tested? I ask as the High Defender. You are my best Warrior pack, Vall. Can she sustain you?"

If it wouldn't have provoked more questions, Vall would have laughed. "That will not be a problem," he said.

Ginn gave him one more searching look, then sighed and stood. "Keep your secrets, then. So long as you continue to do your job, I will be content. I want this saber issue dealt with quickly. I'll expect you to deliver news that they are no longer a threat to the summer house's gods-awful décor imminently." He threw Vall a look. "And if you tell the Sovereign I said that, you'll find yourself his personal bodyguard until you're as old as I am."

Vall gave a small smile as he trailed after Ginn, shortening his steps to match the shuffle of the once virile older man.

"As soon as I have my ma—my thrall settled, I will head over there and look at the situation. A few days at most."

Gill shook his head as he stepped back out into the punishing heat. "No, faster than that. The Sovereign is in a foul mood, and he will be until he knows those responsible are no longer breathing. You'll go today."

"It's already mid-afternoon," Vall complained. "There is no point arriving in darkness."

"First thing tomorrow, then," Ginn replied. "I expect you out of here with the dawn."

Vall gritted his teeth, but he couldn't get around such a precise order, not without a better reason than that he wanted to luxuriate between the sheets with his mate. Especially not when he'd worked so hard to hide her existence.

"Yes, sir," he ground out.

The look Ginn shot him as he clambered back into the vehicle, using Tan and Heo's assistance this time, was full of suspicion.

Vall hadn't completely fooled the High Defender, he knew. Ginn was aware that something was off. "I'll see you soon," he said, as Malin fired up the vehicle. "With good news."

Because he knew it would annoy the old man, Vall gave him a sharp salute. The gesture Ginn threw back was not part of the Warrior training and Vall laughed.

Finn stepped up beside him as soon as the vehicle had lifted off the landing area, taking the High Defender and his entourage out of hearing range.

"What are we going to do?"

Vall shrugged. "Go to the western valley, find the sabers and kill them."

"You know what I mean," Finn groused. "You aren't thinking to take Lana with us?"

Vall growled, his dragon unimpressed at Finn's implication that he would endanger their mate.

"Who is Alpha of this pack?" he asked, teeth drawn back in a display of threat.

Finn held his gaze for longer than Vall expected, then dropped his gaze to glower at the floor. "You are."

"I am," he agreed. "And I make the decisions. Remember that, Finn." He paused. "I'm not going to risk Lana. Jay and Lyne will stay here with her, you and I should be enough to deal with a group of sabers."

It was dicey, taking only half their strength, especially with their thrall so far away if either of them were grievously injured, but Lana wasn't just their blood donor, she was their mate. He would countenance no danger to her, wouldn't take her into such an unknown situation.

Finn nodded, satisfied. "What do you think about the High Defender's theory about the sabers?"

"I think it's possible. They wear clothes, they're starting to develop tools. They understand a few words. But this is a big step up. I don't know, is what I think."

Finn looked thoughtful, his gaze out on the outline of the capital, far off in the distance.

"It puts things in a new perspective, though, doesn't it? What you said, about it making them people, I've been thinking that for a while. And what we're doing, exterminating them—"

"We're doing what we're told," Vall said.

"Is that good enough?" Finn asked softly. A challenge to his Alpha, subtle but there. This time Vall didn't correct him, though, because he was thinking the same thing.

"Come on," he said. "I want to see Lana. We've been away from her for too long."

When they went back into the den, though, things went to hell in the space of a heartbeat. They'd barely made it a step into the hallway leading to Lana's bedroom when Finn, two steps ahead of Vall, stiffened, a growl of outrage rattling up his throat. He took off, out of sight by the time Vall had taken another step forward and realized what had set his Second off — the sweet, sweet scent of their mate's arousal.

Vall made it to the bedroom in time to see Finn tackle Jay, hauling his naked body off the bed and throwing him against the wall. Lyne — also in the bed and also naked — was next, Finn adding insult to injury by punching him in the face before dropping him to the floor. He stood over Lyne, snarling furiously, and the bottom member of the pack, though a strong fighter, was hopelessly out dominated. He stayed down.

Appeased, Finn turned back to Jay, who Vall suspected was the instigator of this little love fest.

"What are they doing?" Lana asked, a fur pulled up to cover her nakedness. This close to her, it was impossible to miss the scent of her pleasure — just as it was impossible to ignore the fact that it was intertwined with Jay and Lyne's. Had they both taken her? If they'd been that stupid, Vall might have to intervene before Finn killed his packmate. Lana's presence in their lives had changed things, raised the stakes.

"It's all right," he murmured, wanting to soothe her. He didn't get on the bed with her and take her in his arms, though, comforting her physically, even though that was what he ached to do. Not when he might have to rescue Jay — who might or might not deserve rescuing.

"You fucking bastard," Finn said, grabbing Jay around the throat as the other Warrior scrambled to get his feet beneath him, pinning him against the wall. "*I'm* second in this pack. It was *my* turn with her."

"I didn't—" Jay gargled, hauling at Finn's crushing grip. He couldn't pull Finn's arm away though. There wasn't much between them in a fair fight, but Finn had the fury of a male wronged to give him strength.

"Liar! I can smell her all over you and I can smell *you* on *her*!"

"We were playing," Jay pleaded. "That's all. We just pleasured her, we didn't fuck her. I swear."

Finn glanced over at Lyne, still on the floor, deliberately staying low, and the bottom member of the pack nodded. "He's telling the truth."

It took a moment, Finn's anger still burning red hot, but eventually he released Jay, letting him slump against the wall as he hauled air into his abused throat.

"You're a motherfucker, Jay. You jumped the hierarchy and you know it."

Jay held his hand up, acknowledging Finn's point. He had that wicked look in his eyes, though and Vall could guess his next comment even before he made it.

"Worth it ,though. You'll know when you have her mouth around your cock."

Lana's small gasp was almost lost beneath the slam of a fist on flesh as Finn hauled back and smashed Jay in the face. This time, when he went down, he stayed down.

CHAPTER THIRTEEN

I stared at the scene in front of me. Lyne was on the floor, his head bowed in submission, and Jay was slumped against the wall, blood dripping from his nose. Finn stood over him, radiating fury, and Vall hovered in front of me, protective but utterly unresponsive to the violence that had just exploded in the room. This was nothing like the sparring I'd watched between the four of them the other day, this was a fight.

Jay's final comment was still ringing in the air and Finn was looking everywhere but at me. I didn't know what to think. On the one hand I was mortified, the fur I'd yanked up when Finn burst into the room the only thing shielding my naked body from view, and even I could smell the scent of sex on the air. Jay and Lyne had jumped the hierarchy, Finn said, which was, given the way he'd tossed Lyne across the room and rung Jay's bell, a bad move.

On the other hand, I was very much not sure I was on board with the whole taking dibs screwing Lana thing. I understood that they were a pack and that was the way they did things, but if I *was* their mate—and I still hadn't reconciled myself to that, wasn't really sure how it differed from being a thrall—then I was part of the pack, and if so, shouldn't how I felt about the situation count, too?

I drew in a shuddering breath. I was angry and confused and yes, a little bit frightened. The violence had been swift and shocking and brutal. It was a different side of the Warriors, Finn in particular, that I hadn't seen before. I didn't like the fact that the fight was over me.

"Get out," I said, the fur clutched tight in my fingers to control my trembling as I gave an order I wasn't at all sure anyone would follow.

Finn turned to look at me then, the expression in his eyes wounded. That just confused me even more.

"Get out," I repeated. I needed some space to think, some room to breathe.

It took a moment, but Finn eventually gave a curt nod and marched out as quickly as he'd stormed in. Jay picked himself up off the floor then. He winced, a hand rubbing at his throat, but the grin he turned on me was arrogant. Smug, even. He took one step toward the bed before I shook my head.

"You, too. You and Lyne. Leave, please."

Lyne left at once, sparing me just one apologetic glance before he scampered, but Jay took a little longer, his lower lip jutting out petulantly.

"You make her ask again, you'll regret it," Vall growled.

It irked me a little that it took Vall's reiteration of my order for Jay to get the message and get out, but he did go. I was finally able to breathe, my shoulders slumping down out of their tense hold.

"I hope you're not going to try to ask me to leave," Vall murmured, turning to me.

I eyed him, standing there, solid as a rock and just as implacable. I'd have better luck trying to move the moon. Besides, I didn't actually want to be alone, not with my thoughts so tangled. The echoes of my orgasm were still singing in my nerves, but the scene that had come afterwards was making me question what we'd done.

"You can stay," I told him softly. I tucked the fur under my arms and looked toward my tunic and trousers, strewn on the floor. "Could you pass me my clothes, please?"

I felt at a disadvantage, bare beneath the feeble protection of the cover. Vall obediently picked them up and handed them to me, turning his back and allowing me to dress in privacy. I appreciated that. I mean, it wasn't anything he hadn't seen before—he was intimately familiar with my body—but at that moment I needed his circumspection.

"Are you going to tell me I did something wrong?" I asked when I was decently covered.

"No." He answered before he turned and when he did, I could see there was a but coming. "You told me where you come, from matings are between a female and a single male."

"Marriages," I muttered.

"We cannot expect you to understand and abide by our ways after a handful of days. The fault is not yours. Jay and Lyne knew what they were doing, and they knew how Finn would feel about it."

"He was so angry," I said doubtfully.

"Not so angry," Vall disagreed. "Jay and Lyne are still alive, aren't they?" When I didn't laugh at his joke, he gave a grim smile and sat down. "The dragon rides us hard, always. Add a new mate into the mix, and skirmishes like this are inevitable. They've fought before and they will again." He gave me a shrewd look. "Did Finn frighten you?"

There was no point lying. I nodded.

"He'll be sorry. Just promise me you'll allow him to explain himself, grovel his way back into your good graces."

"You want me to do that?" I asked. There was only one of me—without Finn, there was less sharing to be done.

"We are a pack," he reminded me. "You accept all of us or none of us."

"I'm still trying to wrap my ahead around that," I confessed.

"Perhaps I have simply not explained it well enough. We are a family, but there is a hierarchy. I am the Alpha, that means what I say goes."

"Does that include me?" I asked teasingly. The smile

dropped from my face somewhat when he nodded.

"You're mine to protect. If I tell you to do something, it's for your safety and I need you to obey. With us, there's less of a choice. Our level of dominance determines our place in the pack. I am the most dominant, so my place is at the top. You saw the way Lyne submitted to Finn?"

I nodded.

"He wasn't hurt, he could have got back up and kept fighting, but he didn't. He knew Finn was the stronger out of the two of them, so he backed down." He paused, giving me a meaningful look. "When it comes to a mate, to you, the hierarchy is even more important. We are all eager to try to convince you that we are a worthy pack and we are all feeling the effects of the dragon within us, pushing to claim you. If we do not obey the chain of command, there will be fighting. You saw what happened, and that was nothing but a little scrap, a warning. If Jay and Lyne do not heed it, the next time there will be blood. Taking a mate is no small thing—it can tear a pack apart."

"So it's you, then Finn, then Jay and then Lyne?" I asked. He nodded. "And once you've gone through the order, do you all, what, take turns? Is there a schedule?" I meant it as a joke, but there was a serious element to my question. "Don't I get a choice?"

"The choice is always yours," Vall told me. "You cannot reject a packmate, that is not fair, but you can dictate which of us you want in your bed." He gave a wicked grin. "Or whether you want all of us."

"All of you?" I squeaked. "I don't think I could handle that."

"You will," he promised. "You'll enjoy it." I eyed him dubiously, but then his salacious expression dropped and he sighed, changing the subject. "There is something I must talk to you about."

"What is it?"

"I have to leave, tomorrow at first light. There is something I have to do for the High Commander." He grimaced. "I had thought to take Finn with me and leave Jay and Lyne to watch over you, but now I think that would not be wise. They will come with me and Finn can remain here." A look out of the corner of his eye. "Perhaps he can prove himself to you."

Vall was about as subtle as a brick. I tried to keep my expression blank, to hide my thoughts, but his words had the intended effect anyway. I was already thinking about it, wondering what it might be like. I'd skipped right over asking myself whether I wanted to.

"I would ask you for something before I go," he went on, and by the slight tensing of his shoulders I could tell this was the thing he'd been building up to.

"Go on," I prompted.

The look he gave me was scorching hot. "The job I must do for the High Defender, it is dangerous. There will be fighting—"

"Maybe you should take Finn with you," I said, concerned. If Finn was his Second, that meant he was his second strongest Warrior.

Vall shook his head. "Jay and Lyne will be more than enough assistance, especially if . . ." he trailed off.

"If?"

"If you would consent to feeding us before we go."

He wanted to drink my blood. To feed from me. A real feeding, not the sips, the little nips at my fingers and my wrist that they'd taken so far. An actual Dracula moment. I drew in a deep breath, somehow more thrown by this idea than I was by a five-way alien orgy. Because really, though it was vastly new territory for me, I'd seen orgies in porn movies back home. People had group sex, they did not go around drinking blood.

But that was, after all, why Vall had chosen me.

"If I do it, if I feed you—" I tripped over the word, "it'll help you fight? Make you stronger?"

Vall closed his eyes briefly, swallowing, and I knew he was imagining it.

"Just the smallest sip from you made me feel invincible," he said. "A full feeding, I cannot imagine the strength it will give me."

"All right, then," I whispered. "I'll do it."

He reached out and cupped my jaw. "And Jay and Lyne, too? You will do the same for my Warriors."

"I will," I promised.

The smile he gave me melted away the uncertainty gripping my chest. "Thank you, little one."

I thought we'd get right down to it then and there, was eager to get it over with because, though I'd agreed, I was definitely still nervous about the idea, but Vall made me wait. He filled Jay and Lyne in on the job, about the sabers who'd desecrated the Sovereign's summer house. I guessed the Sovereign was something like a king, though Vall didn't speak very respectfully about him, not like he did the one he called High Defender. After that, they spent the rest of the day organizing supplies and working out a plan, in between regaling me with stories of their adventures dealing with the sabers, who were a different species but apparently pests who raided communities and stole women and small children. To eat. I think they were trying to allay my fears with their tales, show me that they'd handled this kind of thing dozens of times before, but in reality I was just getting more wound up, although at least some of that was probably because I was waiting for Vall to tell me that it was dinner time, my blood on the menu.

He didn't, though and by the time night had fallen outside and the Warriors were preparing to sleep, ready for their early start the next day, I still hadn't done it.

"Come Lana," Vall said to me, staring at me with hooded eyes. "You need to rest, too."

I stood up off the sofa, but looked uncertainly to Jay and Lyne. "But what about . . ."

"Tomorrow," he said. "Before we go, if you are still willing, Jay and Lyne will drink from you." He turned me toward my bedroom and urged me forward with a hand in the small of my back.

"And you?" I asked quietly, noticing he'd left himself off the list.

He bent down to murmur the words in my ear as we walked. "It is my turn right now."

There was no denying the sexual heat in his voice. I shivered from excitement as much as apprehension. It sounded like feeding time and sexy time were not mutually exclusive. I wasn't sure how I felt about that, but I was prepared to find out.

In my bedroom, Vall didn't waste any time, hands going to my waist as he moved in close behind me, skimming my tunic up and over my head. He snagged my trousers and drew them down my hips, leaving them in a puddle on the floor and me naked as the day I was born.

"Into the bed," he murmured.

I obeyed, keenly aware of what he'd see as I hopped up and crawled into the middle of the mattress on all fours. When I turned around to look at him, his eyes were glowing silver bright, hands at his waist to unbuckle his own trousers. He let them drop and kicked them away from his feet, immediately stalking toward me.

"Am I welcome?" he rasped, halting at the edge of the bed.

I had to lift my gaze from where I'd been staring at his cock, which was already erect, thick and long and pointing toward me eagerly. He was bigger than Jay and Lyne. Alpha cock, I thought, struggling to contain a fit of the giggles.

"Lana?" he prompted, lifting a knee up on to the mattress but coming no further. "Am I welcome?"

I reached for him rather than replying and found myself caught up in his arms a moment later, his weight pushing me back until I lay beneath him, the length of his body hot and hard against mine.

"How does it work?" I asked. "The feeding, I mean."

"I find a vein," he murmured, a hand tracing up my side. "Your wrist, or the inside of you thigh. Your throat."

Right. So really just like a vampire, then.

"Does it hurt?" I sounded scared because I was, my courage deserting me in the face of razor-sharp teeth slicing open one of my arteries.

Vall nuzzled at my nose with his. "I will make sure you are so delirious with pleasure that you don't even notice."

Somehow I doubted that.

"All right," I said, trying to be brave. "Let's do it."

He kissed me once, twice, soft kisses that were little more than a press of his mouth against mine. "Patience, Lana."

He delved deeper then, parting my lips and flicking his tongue into my mouth. I lifted my hands and wound them up into his braided hair, holding him to me. Vall rewarded me by sliding the hand that had been stroking my side in between us and using it to cup my breast, his thumb rubbing idly at my nipple. It was a lazy touch, designed to tease me, and I bucked slightly, wanting more. Wanting something harder. Getting the message, he flicked at the little nub, drawing a gasp from me.

"My mate is demanding," he murmured when I squirmed impatiently against him, wanting him to do it again.

"I'm waiting to be delirious with pleasure," I whispered back cheekily.

It was a dare, and the dragon flared in his eyes as he accepted. I knew what was going to happen a moment before I tasted the iron warmth of his blood on my tongue. He licked at me, filling my mouth, then kissed down my chin and along my throat, encouraging me to swallow. I did, no longer revolted by the thought because I knew what was coming.

A moment later, it started to hit me. My clit pulsed and throbbed, my core aching for something to fill it. My nipples, too, seemed to fill with heat, tightening in preparation for Vall, who'd edged lower until he could graze his teeth over the tips. I moaned, wanting more and he obliged with a lick over my left nipple before nipping his way across to the right and giving it the same treatment.

I could feel how slick I was already, coating Vall's cock and balls as I ground against him, trying to find the right angle to slip him inside. He pulled his hips back, though, frustrating me into giving a little snarl, my pussy clenching almost painfully with the need to come.

"I remember this," he murmured against my breast. "I remember what you like."

He dipped two fingers inside me, allowing me a brief moment of respite from the ache, but then immediately withdrew and lifted them, coated with my arousal, up to my clit.

"Slow and soft, like this. That's how you like it, isn't it?" he asked, drawing circles around my clit that were so light it felt like I was imagining it in my desperate desire to be touched there.

"No," I said, panting now, my hands tight in his hair and twisting hard. "Rougher. Harder. Fuck, Vall, please! More!"

He chuckled. "Are you delirious yet?"

I let go of his braids and smacked at his shoulders, fingers turning into claws and scraping at his back.

He arched into the touch, clearly enjoying it, and then rose up until his face was just above mine. "I think you're ready," he said.

I was about to make a sharp retort when his cock nudged

the entrance to my core. I felt the stretch as he filled me, soothing away the needy cramping. As he slid deeper, he shifted his hand until his thumb was against my clit, pressing harder.

"Oh, yes," I pleaded. "Like that, more like that."

He pushed in until he was as deep as he could go, thumb trapped against my clit by his hips and giving me glorious pressure, then he eased back. At the point he slid home again, his mouth went to my neck. Another glide in and out and I felt the warmth of his tongue on my tender skin. I braced, tightening, fear clawing past my arousal, but when he started to move in a steady rhythm, hips angled to nudge my g-spot, thumb still pressing down on my clit and shifting slightly with every forward slide, I couldn't hold back my orgasm.

Ecstasy swept over me, flooding my system and blanking my thoughts. A sharp, burning pain pierced my pleasure, but a second wave overtook it, transporting me to another plane where the tugging at my neck was little more than a heat, just another place we were connected. I found myself turning into it, cradling his head and trusting him to take care of me as my orgasm left me helpless in its wake.

Shuddering with aftershocks, my pelvic muscles clenching and unclenching around his cock, which had stilled inside me as he'd taken his own release, I felt him pull back and lick at my neck. It stung, but it wasn't as bad as I'd thought. I lifted my hand to feel at the wound, my searching fingers finding only two small punctures that throbbed slightly when I pressed against them.

"Mate," he murmured, nudging my fingers aside so that he could go back to licking at the bite mark, a hand lifting to stroke my forehead and down the side of my face. "My mate. Thank you, Lana. It is a great gift you've given me." He shivered, his breath coming out in a rush as he pressed his face into my hair. "Rest," he told me. "Rest now."

I was lying under him still, his cock thick in my channel,

but as soon as I closed my eyes, darkness claimed me. I slept.

CHAPTER FOURTEEN

Lyne wouldn't look him in the eye and Jay was still pissed. Finn decided he didn't care. They were getting on the hover vehicle, and he was staying. With their mate. Alone.

Lana stood beside him now, her expression uncertain as she watched Vall and Jay pile weapons into the vehicle. She had bandages tied around her wrists from where Jay and Lyne had been allowed to feed from her, a healing mark on her neck proving Vall had done the same last night. It gutted Finn to be the only one who hadn't had a proper taste of her, but he wouldn't swap.

Lana fidgeted as Jay and Lyne climbed on board and Vall approached to bid their mate a final goodbye.

"Are you sure this is going to be safe?" It was at least the fourth time she'd asked the question.

"They'll be fine," Finn replied, resting a hand on her lower back and rubbing gentle, soothing circles. "This is what we do."

"Yes," she said, "but there's usually four of you. Maybe you should go with them?"

"And leave you here alone?"

She bit her lip hesitantly. "I could come."

"No." Vall echoed the word as Finn spoke it, giving Lana a reassuring smile as he closed the last few feet between them. "It warms my heart that you worry for us," he said, "but there's no need."

She nodded, but she didn't look convinced.

"When will you be back?"

Vall shrugged. "By nightfall, hopefully. It depends what we find there, how hard the sabers prove to track. If they've moved off, we might have to hunt them for some time."

"Are you going straight to the Sovereign when you're done?" Finn asked. "I got the feeling Ginn was serious when he said he wanted their skins."

Vall snorted. "He'll just have to be content with knowing they're dead. We'll come straight back here. If the Sovereign wants them so bad, I can leave them in the summer house for him to peruse on his next convalescence."

Finn grinned. "I dare you."

Vall drew Lana into a hug, nuzzling at the top of her head, then he moved back and gave Finn a meaningful look.

Finn nodded, understanding what he was saying. Of course he'd guard their mate.

The hover vehicle finally took off, the three Warriors on board looking back at Lana with undisguised longing until the curve of the land took them out of sight. When it did, she turned to Finn, her smile hesitant and unsure.

He'd frightened her yesterday, and badly. He'd known it even before Vall had hunted him down this morning to tell him so — and demand he fix it.

"So what now?" she asked, fingers nervously plucking at the front of her tunic.

"We can do whatever you want," Finn replied smoothly. "Do you want to eat, or walk in the garden? Bathe?" An image of Lana, wet and gleaming from the water, slipped unbidden into his mind and the last word came out more of a growl. She blanched, shaking her head.

Yeah, he definitely had work to do.

"Can we go into the city?" she asked, her cute, furry little brows lifting up hopefully. They fell with disappointment when he had to shake his head.

"Anything but that," he said regretfully. "We will take you, and soon, but now that you've been marked—" He reached up to trace the seven improbable stars decorating her cheek, identifying her as the miracle she was, "it's not safe to take you into such a populated area without the four of us to protect you."

"People would try to hurt me?" she asked, forehead scrunching up in confusion.

"They might try to take you from us. At the very least, they'd spread news of your existence, and we aren't ready for anyone else to know yet, not until we understand more about your blood and what it's doing to us."

"I don't really understand that either," she said helplessly.

Finn grimaced, not sure how much to say. Vall hadn't told him to keep this secret, but if he hadn't told her himself . . .A look in her eyes, though, wide and beseeching, and Finn knew he couldn't deny her.

"We have a dragon inside us," he said. "It's strongest in Warriors, and that's why we need blood, to keep it satiated."

She nodded. "Vall told me that."

"Our ancestors were able to become the dragon, shift into enormous creatures that could take to the skies, break our enemies in half with one snap of their teeth."

"He told me that, too," she said, though her expression told Finn she was skeptical. It was understandable. This was Finn's history, and yet even he almost couldn't imagine it.

"Our females' blood is no longer strong enough to bring forth the dragon in our Warriors. We don't know why, or what happened. But *your* blood . . ." He tailed off.

She eyed him dubiously. "You think I could be the key to unlocking your dragon?"

It was Finn's turn to nod. "Vall said he could feel it inside him, stirring. Striving to break free."

"That's, well, that's unbelievable."

"Do you understand now why we must be cautious? You

could change the course of my race's entire future."

"But there's only one of me," she argued.

"Yes," he said, "and you're ours. But if it's true that you can unleash our beasts, there is not a Warrior on the planet who wouldn't steal or kill or commit any other crime, just to have you."

She took a long, silent moment to reflect, then quirked a small smile. "So no to the city then?"

"I'm afraid not," he replied. "Though, if you want to get out of here, see some of the countryside, we could take the skimmer. There's a beautiful lake nearby, and I could pack food for lunch?"

"A picnic?" Lana asked, looking eager.

"A picnic," he agreed, even though he wasn't sure exactly what that was.

It didn't take long to organize a bag of food. He had Lana wait on the landing pad with it while he accessed the garage cleverly concealed underneath and brought out the skimmer.

"It's like a motorcycle," she said nervously, eyeing the vehicle as he brought it in to land beside her.

"You have something like this where you're from?" he asked.

"Kind of," she replied, making a face. "On Earth, a motorcycle has wheels, it doesn't float off the ground like that, but otherwise yeah, I guess it's pretty much the same."

He took the bag of food from her and stored it in the skimmer's saddle bag, then held out a hand.

"Put your foot here," he said, tapping on the footrest at the bottom of the skimmer with his boot, "then swing your other leg up and over."

She looked a little apprehensive but did as he said, though she was so small she struggled to get her leg high enough to clear the skimmer's seat.

"You'll want to put your arms around my waist," he told

her once she was perched on the vehicle behind him. "Scoot in close to me. It'll protect you from the air drag. The automatic shield doesn't always protect you in the back."

She slid up behind him, and Finn fought to repress the shudder as he felt her inner thighs slide along the outside of his legs, her heat all the way down his back. She was wearing a full sleeved tunic, so they weren't skin to skin, but her hands fluttered across his stomach, the ticklish touch causing his muscles to clench. He'd never ridden with anyone else on the back of the skimmer before, and after having his mate cling to him so sweetly, he didn't think he'd ever allow anyone else to do so again.

"Are you ready?" he asked. "You'll need to hold tight, it's faster than the hover vehicle."

That was all the warning he gave her before he gunned the skimmer, sending it shooting off the landing pad and straight down the hill. Hot air blasted him, lifting his braids and stinging his eyes, but he barely felt it, his full concentration on Lana's hands gripping the belt of his trousers, just a couple of inches above his quickly stiffening cock, as she cuddled in as tight as she could, squealing every time he made a minute adjustment to the skimmer's controls.

"Are you all right?" he called.

It took a moment, but eventually she gave a muffled, "Yes."

"Do you want to go faster?" He grinned as he said it, predicting the way her hands clasped immediately tighter.

"No! I feel like I'm going to fall off!"

"I won't let you fall," he vowed.

Remembering his promise to let her take in the landscape—and that he was supposed to be making her *less* afraid of him, not more—he slackened off the pace as they reached the valley floor and started heading south toward the lake. It was a long drive, but the road followed alongside the river, whose cooling waters kept the air from getting too hot and dry. There was no one around, either, the quiet helping Finn to relax. They weren't a populous people, and the invention of the transporters had given them the ability to spread more widely across the habitable areas of the planet. Most still chose to congregate in the cities—because they might not be many, but they were sociable creatures, the Thinkers and Artists especially—which meant the ones like Finn and his pack, who chose a rural dwelling, could be as isolated as they pleased.

While they hadn't gone quite as far as Bern and Danin in isolating themselves, it was nice to know that Finn could take Lana out to enjoy the countryside without expecting to run into—

Finn's thoughts broke off as a something caught his attention in the periphery of his vision. He slowed the skimmer, head turning toward the tree line where he thought he'd seen something moving, something not quite right. Though he squinted against the sun's glare, he didn't catch it again, that spark of light on metal that had no place in the dense foliage.

"Is everything all right?" Lana asked, feeling the deceleration and, probably, the sudden tension in Finn. He made himself relax his muscles and gave a short shrug.

"Fine," he said. "I just thought I saw something. It was probably an animal. There's quite a lot of wildlife in this region."

"Dangerous wildlife?" she asked nervously.

He turned his head enough to show her a flash of his fangs. "Nothing as dangerous as me."

"There aren't any of those saber things around here, are there?"

"No," he said. "They'd never nest within our territory."

"How do they know it's your territory?"

"We mark it," he said simply.

There was a brief pause then Lana said, voice tight, "I don't think I'm going to ask how you do that."

Finn laughed — because they did exactly what he thought Lana was imagining, leaving their scent by pissing on trees all around the perimeter — and thumbed the accelerator down on the skimmer, speeding up once more.

Though he kept a sharp eye out, he didn't see anything like that strange flash again, and by the time they reached the point where the river slid into the calm of the lake, he'd just about convinced himself that he'd imagined it. Still, he took a good long look at the forest, which had followed them all this way and now spread out in a curve around the lake's edge, even going so far as to mark against a tree nearby in case any predators — imaginary sabers or otherwise — got curious and came to investigate.

"This is beautiful," Lana said, her gaze drawn to the shimmering surface of the lake as she lingered by the skimmer.

"It is," Finn agreed, his gaze on her.

It took her a little while to see what — who — he was looking at as he spoke, and when she did, she rolled her eyes.

"I was talking about the view!"

"So was I," he said innocently, pulling out the food bag. "Are you hungry now, or do you want to swim first?"

"Swim?" she said, looking surprised. "But I didn't bring a swimsuit."

"Neither did I."

She gave him a sideways glance, a warning to behave, but she was smiling, and there was a red tint to her cheeks. Finn slid a few steps closer and inhaled discreetly. No sense of fear, either. Good. He didn't seem to have damaged things between them permanently.

"You're warm," he murmured, running the backs of his fingers down her neck where sweat was making little tendrils of hair stick to her skin. "The water's lovely and cool."

She was considering it, her teeth chewing on her bottom lip in indecision, but then she shook her head and took the bag of food from him.

"Food first," she said. "I'm hungry."

Disappointed, but not deterred — because she'd said food *first* — Finn followed her to the edge of the water and sat down with her on a patch of thick grass.

"We should have brought a blanket," she said ruefully, diving into the bag.

"To lie on?" Finn asked suggestively.

This time he got a smack on the arm and a "Behave!" for his trouble. He grinned. She was losing her wariness of him more quickly than he'd feared.

They ate in companionable quiet, enjoying listening to the gentle lap of the water and the occasional call of creatures within the trees. Lana asked him about some of the plants, the forest and the things that lived there, and although Finn was pretty knowledgeable about things with teeth, he was admittedly hopeless when it came to things that flowered.

"We can get you a book," he said, "and you can learn about them, if you're interested."

"When I'm finally allowed to go to the city?"

"When it is safe to go," he agreed.

She gave a nod and stood up. Leaning back on his elbows, Finn glanced at the tree line again, as he'd done a dozen times while they ate. Something shifted there, a shadow. It was likely an animal, he told himself, though it was large. There were grazers who came down to the lake to drink, that was probably all it was. He was staring hard into the thick greenery, trying to decide whether he needed to get up and investigate, or whether he was just being paranoid, when Lana suddenly whipped her tunic up and off.

Finn froze, stunned, his gaze hopelessly drawn to the sleek lines of her back and the hint of curved breast he could see, when she slipped her trousers off with the same decisive movements, revealing shapely legs and a deliciously rounded backside. Before he could get himself together enough to reach for her, she was gone, running the few steps into the water and then wading deeper. She squealed as the cold water tickled around her legs then, as it reached her hips, she dove, disappearing beneath the surface entirely.

Finn was on his feet in a heartbeat, his gut clenching as he stared at the empty water. The ripples she'd caused ebbed into flat calm and still she didn't reappear. He'd just splashed into the shallows, boots and trousers and all, when two things happened simultaneously. Lana popped up much deeper in the lake, grinning, her hair slicked back against her head, and a group of six Warriors emerged from the trees.

Caught between his mate and a strange pack whose narrowed eyes and exposed fangs told Finn they weren't friendly, he immediately looked to the skimmer. It was fast, easily quick enough to get away from the Warriors on foot, but even if they had vehicles hidden in the bushes, they'd never catch him. Lana was too deep in the water, though. By the time she got to the shore, it'd be too late.

"Lana, stay there!" he shouted, then he turned to face the threat.

"Finn?" she called, fear tingeing his name. He glanced at her and saw her swimming hesitantly back toward him, worry written all over her face.

"Stay. There!" he repeated.

He had to trust she'd obey his word this time, because he didn't dare take his attention off the Warriors again. They were advancing slowly, watching for any move Finn might make, though they had him easily outnumbered. He couldn't hope to win a fight against the six of them.

"Who are you?" he snarled, flashing his own fangs. "This is our territory."

"You say *our*," one of them threw back, a big Warrior with his head shaved and ragged scar down one pectoral. "And yet it's only you."

"It's pack territory," he spat.

"But there's no pack." The big Warrior grinned. Then his gaze went to Lana, dismissing Finn. "Seven stars," he murmured. "Impossible."

Lana was too far out in the water for the Warrior to be able to count the small marks on her cheek, which meant he knew. It meant he'd come here for her specifically. Finn's stomach twisted, the dragon in his chest going crazy with the desire to get out, but it didn't have the strength. There was no push against his skin, just terror in his heart.

"Are you going to come out, female?" the Warrior called. "Or do I have to come in there and get you?" He licked his lips as he said it, his expression hungry. Finn snarled and shifted position, getting in the Warrior's line of sight and hiding Lana from view.

It was impossible odds, he knew that. If they'd stayed at the den, been ambushed there, there were places he could have retreated to with Lana, barricaded them in until the rest of the pack returned to even things up, but here he was exposed and vulnerable. Still, he wasn't going down without a fight.

"She's mine," he snarled. "Don't touch her."

The big Warrior considered him briefly. "Then you should have taken more care with her." He signaled with his hand at the other five Warriors, waiting restlessly. "Get him out of the way."

Finn waited until they were halfway to him, then exploded out of the water. He had the element of surprise, the Warriors expecting him to yield to the inevitable, and he was able to take the first one down with a vicious strike to the throat, a second falling as he kicked out, feeling ribs crack beneath his foot. He had a third by the throat when an arm wrapped around him from behind, choking him. A hard hit to his thigh had his leg collapsing beneath him and putting more pressure on his neck. Finn twisted and writhed, letting go of the Warrior in front to claw at the arm strangling him, but that just left another enemy to rain down blows.

Though he fought as hard as he could, there were too many of them. Eventually they were able to muscle him to his knees and pull both arms behind his back, thick manacles encircling his wrists and keeping them there. Fettered and powerless, he could only watch as the lead Warrior waded into the water toward Lana. She, too, tried to fight, water splashing as she flailed against him, but it was almost too easy for him to scoop her up. Finn got one glance at her naked body, held tightly against the Warrior's chest as they emerged from the lake, before a sharp blow to the back of his head turned everything black.

CHAPTER FIFTEEN

An Administrator met them at the entrance to the summer house, clothed in long, flowing silks that skimmed her willowy frame. Her eyes were overlarge in her slightly narrowed face, her expression uncertain as she wrung her hands with agitation.

"Do you want to come in?" she asked, gesturing to the open door behind her. "See what they did?"

Vall nodded and he, Jay and Lyne trooped in behind the female. The place was beautifully decorated, the walls hung with art and fancy bits of furniture placed in odd corners where no one would ever actually want to sit. The rancid stink of saber piss killed the ambience the designer had been going for, though. It hung heavy in the air, getting stronger as they moved into a drawing room that looked as if it had been the epitome of high society before a plague of mangy cats had come in and destroyed everything.

"It's just awful," the Administrator said, a handkerchief held up to cover her mouth and nose. She looked like she was about to cry. "Why would they do this?"

"They're animals," Jay muttered. "They don't have to have a reason. They just act."

Maybe. Vall wasn't convinced of that, not after what Ginn had said and what he'd witnessed with his own eyes, but the Administrator nodded, unhappy but appeased.

"You'll be able to catch them, won't you?" she asked. "Bring them to justice?"

Vall stared at her, incredulous. "We'll kill them," he said.

"Oh." She looked shocked, then stricken, but a glance at the mess, at the clawed walls and tattered remains of the soft furnishing, stiffened her spine. "Well, I suppose that's what has to be done. I mean, this is the Sovereign's summer house! Have they no respect?"

Vall turned his back on the female so he wouldn't make the caustic comment lingering on his tongue. Was a little vandalism worth a life? A handful of lives? He picked up a throw pillow tossed carelessly on the floor, the intricate embroidery shredded until the pattern was unrecognizable. He lifted it to his face and sniffed deeply. Two different scents, both male. Satisfied, he tore a patch free.

"What are you doing?" the Administrator asked, scandalized.

Vall eyed her over his shoulder. She was upset that he'd torn an already ruined pillow?

"Scents," he said simply.

She didn't look impressed, but she held her tongue as he and Jay and Lyne went around the room. By the time they'd finished, Vall reckoned he was going hunting for a group of at least six sabers.

"Thank you," he said to the female. "We have what we need now."

They started to head toward the door when she gave a strangled little squawk. "You're leaving? What if they come back? Shouldn't one of you stay here? Hello?"

Vall ignored her, walking back out into the sunshine. Once there, he breathed deeply, wanting to wash the stink out of his nose.

"You want me to stay? In case they do circle back here and attack?" Lyne asked.

"Fuck no," Vall replied. "That Administrator is not our problem."

"Really? This is what we're going to talk about?" Jay asked.

"No one's going to bring up the big problem we just uncovered?"

"What problem?" Lyne asked, looking to Vall and frowning.

"One of the sabers is different. The scent —"

Vall handed Lyne a torn scrap of wallpaper. He watched as Lyne held it up to his face and drew in the scent. Vall could actually see the confusion form behind his eyes.

"I don't understand."

"I don't either," Vall replied.

"It's one unique scent," Jay stated. "It isn't two individuals."

"I know," Vall said.

"How can that be?"

Vall shrugged. It was unbelievable, but there was only one answer. "Hybrid."

"What?" Lyne gasped. "Is that even possible?"

"When we find the sabers, I guess we'll know."

The trail the sabers left was almost too easy to believe. If they had been Warriors, Vall would have said they wanted to be followed. The skeptic inside him whispered that their total lack of care in hiding their tracks just proved that they were nothing but dumb beasts, but he tried to quiet that voice. Ginn had sent him here to deal with a problem, but also to listen and observe. He needed to leave his prejudices behind.

They headed into the dense greenery behind the summer house, following a passage of broken twigs, trampled grass, and footprints sunk deep into the cloying mud. At one point the sabers had crossed a narrow river, choosing a stony spot Vall would have taken himself, a good move if they hadn't signposted their crossing by leaving a torn snag of fabric on a low-hanging branch.

"How long ago were the sabers at the summer house?"

Lyne asked as Vall snagged the fabric and sniffed at it to confirm it had come from one of the scents they were chasing. It had. "Days? They could be anywhere by now."

"You don't really think they've hung about, do you?" Jay asked. "I don't want to be out here forever—I want to get back to Lana."

"We follow the tracks until we find something," Vall said firmly. "It takes as long as it takes. Which will be longer if I have to listen to the pair of you whining every five minutes. Are you Warriors or not?"

"I'm a mated Warrior who hasn't gotten to mate with his mate yet," Jay muttered, but low enough that Vall could choose to ignore it.

"I have a feeling they haven't gone far," he said quietly, staring off into the trees.

"Why would they stick around?" Lyne asked.

"I don't know," he said. Dropping the scrap of fabric, he scrambled out of the riverbank and continued following the tracks. They hadn't gone much further, had only been hiking through the forest for half an afternoon, when a much fresher scent made Vall stop dead. It was one of the males who'd been in the summer house, but the tree he'd marked was still wet with his piss. He'd been here recently. Very recently.

Silently, Vall dropped into a crouch, Jay and Lyne following suit behind him. He listened hard, keen eyes searching, but nothing moved or made a sound.

"Lyne, east. Jay, you head west. I'll keep going north. If they're still here, they've made a camp. You find it, you head back here. If you haven't found anything within an hour, start backtracking."

The two Warriors nodded and Vall lingered as he watched them disappear. He waited until he was sure they were out of earshot before saying quietly, "You can come out now."

It took a moment, but eventually the foliage in a tree just a few feet ahead began to rustle as a small figure scrambled out of it. It used the tree's trunk to hide from view, two big, frightened eyes peering round at Vall.

"It's all right," he said. "I won't hurt you."

He hadn't been sure, the little urchin hadn't done anything to give himself away, even the wind direction had worked in his favor, but Vall had sensed it, the presence of another dragon. Jay and Lyne hadn't, but they weren't Alpha in the pack for a reason. The dragon wasn't as strong in them.

Except, as the child, less than half grown, perhaps eight summers old, stepped out from behind the tree with slow, hesitant steps, he saw it wasn't a dragon after all. There was dragon in there, it was evident in the eyes, in the quiet watchfulness and the tell-tale slitted pupils, but the boy also had a downy fur covering his body and there, flicking between his legs, a tail. He was a hybrid. A mix of dragon and saber.

"You're not supposed to be out here, are you?" he asked quietly.

The boy hesitated, then shook his head.

"Where's the rest of your group?"

Another hesitation, longer this time, then he lifted a trembling arm and pointed north.

"I think we should take you back there, little one." Standing to his full height with careful, unhurried movements, he moved forward slowly. The child didn't bolt, just watched him with those huge eyes. "What's your name?"

The boy frowned, lips moving. At first Vall thought he was going to refuse, but then he realized he was just struggling to wrap his mouth around the word he wanted to say. His lips, like the sabers', weren't formed quite right for easy speech.

"Kell," he finally got out, the 'k' sound slightly mangled.

"Kell?"

The boy nodded.

"All right then, Kell. Let's you and I go back to your

group."

They started walking, Vall deliberately making enough noise to give away his passage. He didn't want to surprise them, have them spring into attack with the child in the middle of the fracas.

"Tell me," he said, speaking pleasantly, as if the question was of no importance. "Have you met anyone who looks like me before?" Kell stared up at him, uncertain. "My skin," he clarified. "My eyes."

A nod, barely there.

"Your father?" Kell shook his head no. "Your mother?"

Kell bit his lip worriedly.

Had he been told not to speak about it? Maybe he was just wary of strangers, especially ones who had been sent to kill him.

"Don't be afraid," Vall soothed. "You aren't in trouble. I look like your mother, yes?"

"Isss," Kell agreed.

"Is she here, your mother?"

"Nuh."

"You came with your father?"

"Isss."

So there was a female dragon breeding with the sabers— voluntarily or not, he'd no idea. She wasn't here, though, so this wouldn't be a rescue mission. He thought of the stories the villagers had told him just a handful of days ago, when he'd gone to clear out the nest that was terrorizing them, stealing and damaging, kidnapping young women. The villagers had been hysterical, claiming the sabers were eating the ones they stole. Apparently, the sabers had other plans for them.

He knew when they were approaching the camp. The sabers' scents were rich in the air, but they were also noisy, laughing and jabbering at each other. When Vall broke through the final few trees blocking them from view, he saw three of them sitting in a semicircle watching two who had sharpened sticks and were fencing with each other, the engagement light-hearted, smiles on both their faces. He dropped a hand on Kell's shoulder, holding back the boy when he would have run to rejoin his family. A moment later, the sabers realized he was there and the pretend fighting stopped instantly.

The three on the ground scrambled to their feet, joining the two holding sticks in a line of aggression that vibrated with unhappy growls. They didn't rush forward in attack, though, because Kell, who was trembling now, terrified to be trapped in the middle, was close enough to Vall for him to easily reach out and snap the boy's neck before any of the sabers could reach him.

He wouldn't, but they didn't know that.

"I found this wandering the forest," he said, slowly and clearly. "He belongs to one of you?"

The snarls rumbled loudly, but then one of the sabers stepped forward. It was one of the two bearing sticks. He dropped it quickly to the ground and held his hands out, eyes cautious.

"Mine," he said. "Give."

Kell tried to run to his father, but Vall clung on. He needed the boy as leverage, because even with Lana's blood pulsing through his veins, making him feel invincible, taking five sabers on by himself after he'd threatened one of their young, was asking a lot. Perhaps he had been hasty sending Lyne and Jay away, but he hadn't thought the little one would come to him otherwise.

"Not yet," he said, wanting to be clear that he *was* going to hand Kell over, but not before they had a little chat. Kell's father shifted restlessly, clawed toes digging into the mossy forest floor.

"Give," he repeated. Then, as if it were dragged from him,

"Pleasssse."

"Soon," Vall promised. "The damage to the summer palace, the big house. That was you?"

Kell's father looked back toward the rest of the sabers, some unspoken communication passing between them. A second saber stepped forward. This one was older, grey dappling his muzzled mouth. His eyes were shrewd, hard.

"Deserved it," he spat.

"Do you know whose house it was?" Vall asked.

"SSSSovereign." It was hard for the saber to spit out the title, but he still managed to infuse it with distain. If he hadn't been so astounded, Vall might have smiled. That was exactly the tone he used whenever he referred to their glorious king.

"Why? Why did he deserve it?"

"Hunts us," the saber growled. "Hurts us. Won't let us be."

"Maybe he would if you weren't stealing his females," Vall pointed out, though he knew even as he said it that this wasn't true. The Sovereign was determined to hunt the sabers to extinction no matter what.

"Not stealing," the older saber replied, outraged.

Vall tilted his head down toward Kell, who was ignoring the conversation, utterly focused on the father he was desperate to run to.

The father, however, was looking even more unhappy about the direction the conversation was taking.

"Mine," he insisted. "My Jalla. My mate. Not take her."

Mate? That put a different spin on things, providing sabers saw mates in the same way as dragons did, which was impossible to know.

"But does she want to be your mate?" Vall asked quietly.

The saber frowned, a frustrated whine coming from his throat as he pawed at the ground.

"My mate," he repeated. "My Jalla."

He might have been irritated by the question, or maybe he

just didn't understand. The rest of the sabers in the background were getting restless, teetering on the edge of breaking down into violence. Vall didn't want that.

Jay and Lyne were nearby now, both of them having circled in to find the camp. They were waiting and watching, looking for a signal from their Alpha. If it came to it, Vall knew they'd be able to take the group, even outnumbered almost two to one. But if the fighting started, it would be to the death. Vall wouldn't kill Kell, which meant he'd be leaving the child fatherless, would have to choose between abandoning him in the forest to fend for himself, or taking him back to the city, to the High Defender and the Sovereign and have everyone treat him like a freak, a science experiment.

Time to go. He had enough to take back to the High Defender anyway.

"I haven't hurt the boy," he said, taking his hand off Kell's shoulder, "and I haven't hurt you." He made a discreet gesture with his hand, and Jay and Lyne stepped forward, just far enough for the sabers to see them, to realize he wasn't here alone. "I'm going to give you back your child, then I'm going to leave. If you try to stop me, you're going to die. Do you understand?"

The father looked faint with relief. He dropped to his knees, arms outstretched in a silent plea for his child. It was the older one Vall looked to, though. When he gave a brief nod, Vall nudged the boy toward his father. He'd turned and started walking away before Kell had even begun running.

He kept a careful watch on Jay and Lyne, not far behind him, watching their expressions so he'd know if he was about to experience an attack from behind. Their faces remained neutral as they backed away in tandem with Vall's steps. They didn't turn their backs on the sabers until they'd put a good distance between them.

"We're leaving them alive?" Lyne asked. "I thought the job

was to take out the nest. Isn't the Sovereign expecting to see bodies?"

"We're not killing anyone," Vall said. "If the Sovereign wants them dead, he can come out here and do it himself. We need to report to the High Defender though. I've got news for him."

"I'll say," commented Jay. "Did I see what I thought I saw?"

"You did," Vall confirmed. "But there's more. The High Defender was right, they did specifically target the Sovereign's palace. They want him to stop harassing them, leave them in peace."

"That's not going to happen so long as they're stealing females and breeding with them!" Jay exclaimed.

"*If* they're stealing females," Vall replied. It had been his first thought too, but perhaps he was as wrong about that as he had been about the sabers being unintelligent, mindless beasts. The whole thing was a nightmare. Fuck, how many of them had he killed?

No, if they were people, the word was *murdered*.

"This is a mess," Lyne commented.

Val snorted. That was an understatement.

They were almost back to the hover vehicle when the fear hit him like a bolt of lightning. He stopped dead, surprising Jay and Lyne who kept going for several more paces before looking back at him.

"What is it?" Jay asked. He glanced over Vall's shoulder. "Is it the sabers? Do you think they're following us? I don't see anything."

"Lana," Vall gasped.

He didn't know why he knew it—dragons weren't psychic—but his blood was screaming with the truth of it. Lana was afraid, she was in trouble.

Jay and Lyne were speaking, asking him questions, but he

couldn't hear them. The dragon inside him was roaring in his mind so loud it was deafening. It was clamoring at him, demanding to be set free so it could follow the call of Vall's blood thrumming in her veins. It could find her, it insisted.

Frozen with terror for the first time in his life, Vall capitulated, stepping back and letting the dragon come to the fore. It surged forward with a fury, tearing open his skin and doubling, tripling, quadrupling in size. Vall's thoughts diminished, over-written by the simple needs of the dragon.

Mate. Scared. Find.

Scaled feet the size of a skimmer pushing hard against the ground, Vall's dragon launched them upward, into the sky.

CHAPTER SIXTEEN

Finn wouldn't wake up. I sat on the chair where the terrifying Warrior with the big scar running across his chest had dumped me and stared across the room to where Finn was slumped on the floor. One of the Warriors stood over him, lip curled back in disdain, and as I watched, he kicked him hard in the ribs with a booted foot, one hand gripping his own side.

Finn still didn't stir.

"He dead?" A third Warrior called. "You kill him when you cracked his skull?"

My heart jumped into my throat until the Warrior shook his head. "No, he's breathing. I should have, though. He's broken my ribs."

He pulled his boot back to aim another kick.

"Leave him alone!" My voice rang out, loud in the space. It drew me to the attention of all six of the very scary, strange men surrounding me, but at least the asshole with the broken ribs stepped away without kicking Finn again.

Unfortunately, a moment later the scarred Warrior was back, hunkering down in front of me.

"You don't need to worry about him anymore," he told me. "You belong to us now."

"I don't fucking think so," I hissed. I was furious, but I was also shit-scared, and when he shifted slightly on the balls of his feet, I slammed backward, thinking he was going to hit me.

He didn't, he just lifted his hand up to my face, tucking my hair behind my ear and revealing the stars on my cheek.

"Seven stars," he murmured, shaking his head. "I'm looking at it and I still can't believe it. Maybe what I need to do is taste." He lingered over the last word, letting it roll across his tongue.

I drew back, almost toppling over my chair in my desperation to get away. "Don't touch me!"

"I will touch you, and more," he promised. "You're going to be our thrall, little one. You need to get used to that idea. If you won't do it voluntarily, I'll make you, and I don't think you'd like that." He gave a soft smile that didn't reach his eyes. "Maybe you just need a little while to get used to the idea, huh? Time to settle in. You can have that, but my patience is not limitless. I suggest you not test it."

He stood up and stroked down my hair. I wanted to jerk my head away, but I made myself sit still, not wanting to antagonize him. I thought perhaps that might have been the wrong move when he clucked approvingly and crooned, "Good girl." I wasn't his good girl, I wasn't his anything, and I tried to convey that to him when I flashed my eyes at him angrily, but he'd already turned away from me.

Feeling isolated and very much alone, I looked around. We'd travelled here on a hover vehicle, the passenger area tightly packed with the six Warriors, me and Finn's limp body. The skimmer had been trashed and left by the lake. I'd no idea what direction we'd travelled in, hadn't recognized any of the countryside, but eventually the Warrior driving steered the hover off the wide-open road and onto a track where branches whipped at the side of the vehicle as we zoomed along. We'd gone deep into the trees until we'd come to a squat, square building with no windows. There hadn't been a front door, either, just a garage that opened as we'd approached so the driver had been able to take the hover right inside.

I'd expected a tomb-like interior, given the lack of

windows, but the wide, open living space that I'd been carried into — where I was still seated now — was bright and sunny, huge skylights letting sunlight dapple through the trees that grew so close to the walls of the building that their canopy spread right over the top of it. It was beautiful, and I'd have appreciated it if I hadn't been dragged here against my will.

I wasn't tied down, but I didn't dare leave my chair. The Warriors moved around me, patching themselves up after the fight with Finn, who'd managed to do quite a lot of damage against the five who had attacked him. There was a ruckus in the corner as a squabble broke out between two of them, fists flying until the Warrior with the scar — the Alpha, I presumed — waded over to break it up, flinging them both apart.

"Knock it off," he said. He glanced over at me, smirking. "See what you're doing to them, sweetheart? They're fighting to move up the ranks, desperate to get their hands on you."

I looked away, biting back all the scathing comments I wanted to hurl at him. My gaze fell on Finn and I gave a startled gasp. He was lying immobile on the floor still, his limbs sprawled at uncomfortable angles, but his eyes were open and staring at me. I opened my mouth, but before I could do anything stupid like draw attention to him, he shook his head, warning me to keep silent. He shut his eyes again a moment later, when the Alpha, done with disciplining his unruly pack members, wandered over to him. He leaned down and grabbed Finn's braid, yanking his head back. It must have hurt, but Finn continued playing dead, his body lax and face expressionless.

"What are we going to do with this one, eh?" he mused. I saw him glance at me askance and knew he was trying to goad me. Though my heart was hammering with fright for Finn, I managed to stay where I was, my mouth firmly closed.

"We should kill him," commented one of the two that had been wrestling, wiping blood from his mouth as he got to his feet.

The Alpha considered the suggestion, then shook his head. "I don't want a war with Vall's pack."

Someone snorted. "We've kidnapped his thrall, we're going to have a war."

"They can have our thrall. That's fair. A female for a female."

"Our thrall isn't even marked," another of them drawled. "I doubt he'll see it as a fair trade."

"And what's he going to do about it? You think his pack is going to be able to take us on when we're feeding from a seven-star female? It would be suicide. No Warrior is going to die for a thrall, no matter how many stars she has."

"I'm not their thrall," I said quickly. "I'm their mate."

Mate. I'd panicked when Vall had thrown that word at me the first time. I was using it now to try and make them understand how serious the situation was. I hoped Vall and the rest of the pack wouldn't die for me, but I knew they'd never give up.

"Another reason to kill him," the one with the cracked ribs said, sending Finn a filthy look and cradling his side. "Think how much we'd weaken them if we took out their Second."

"I'm not killing him," the Alpha growled. "The High Defender might overlook a bit of thrall swapping, but if we start murdering his Warriors, we'll have every pack on the planet at our throats."

"If she's telling the truth and she's their mate, he won't overlook that."

"If," the Alpha scoffed. He tilted his head and looked at me. "She's not pregnant, I'd have smelled it. But she could be." A slow, unpleasant smile crept across his face. "Maybe it's time we took a mate."

Finn flinched then, I saw it, but the Alpha's attention was too fixed on me to notice.

"I won't be your mate," I said tersely, trying to keep his attention in my direction.

"We'll see," he said. He let go of Finn's hair and flung him back to the floor. I winced as his temple connected with the tiling with a sickening thud.

The Alpha left the room then, stalking out down a corridor. As soon as he was out of sight, the atmosphere changed. I felt it, a hunger, a threat hanging in the air. The Warriors were all watching me from various points around the room. They'd been behaving before because the Alpha was there to make them. Now . . .

What was the expression—it was easier to ask for forgiveness than permission? They were thinking about touching me, and they were thinking about hurting Finn. Their Alpha would be mad later, but the damage would still be done.

Feeling vulnerable on my chair and even more worried about Finn—I couldn't tell if he was pretending to be unconscious, or whether he really was knocked out again after the Alpha Warrior smacked his head off the ground—I inched forward until I was perched right on the edge of my seat. No one said anything and no one moved in my direction. They just continued to watch me hungrily.

I stood up and took a step toward Finn, then another. When I didn't hear a shout or feel a hand wrap around my arm in restraint, I grew both braver and more desperate, scurrying across the space until I was able to crash to my knees in front of Finn. My hand went straight to his temple, feeling at the bump that was already swelling up.

"Are you okay?" I whispered as quietly as I could. I wasn't sure how good their hearing was—except that it was better than mine—and I didn't want to be overheard. I didn't know that I'd even said it loud enough for Finn to hear me, but I thought I saw his head shift ever so slightly. A nod.

I hoped.

I ran my hands over his braided hair, tears stinging in my eyes. I'd no idea what to do, how to help. We were hopelessly outnumbered, and I didn't know how to contact Vall and the others to even things out a little. I was fairly sure this new pack wouldn't hurt me — much — because they needed my blood, though I supposed I'd bleed just as well willing or un-willing. If the Alpha was truthful about wanting me as a mate, I thought I'd be able to buy a little time before I was in physi-cal danger. Finn, though . . .no matter what the Alpha said, I knew there were Warriors in the room who thought it'd be easier if he was dead.

I itched at the bandage around my left wrist, the wound where Jay had fed from me this morning stinging slightly. Glancing down, I saw spots of red dotting through. I must have torn it open in the lake when I was struggling against the Alpha.

I hadn't done very well. He'd subdued me with pathetic ease.

Something sparked in my mind, a comment Vall made last night before he fed from me. *Just the smallest sip from you made me feel invincible . . .A full feeding, I cannot imagine the strength it will give me.*

Would it be enough for Finn to fight off the pack, get away so that he could raise the alarm? If I stayed here, if they had me, maybe they wouldn't bother to chase him?

I'd no way to communicate to Finn what I was thinking. The Warriors around us were sure to notice if I started whis-pering to him furiously. Instead, I touched his cheek briefly to get his attention. Shifting my weight to hide my hands, I started working at the knot keeping my bandage tied.

"Aw, look, she's stroking him," one said from across the room. "I hope she looks after us like that. Can't even get a blow job from our thrall."

There was a titter of laughter, and I turned to glower at the room. In reality, I was making sure they stayed put while I pulled the bandage free and held my wrist up to Finn's mouth. He twisted away slightly when I put my bloodied flesh to his lips, but I followed the movement, pushing harder. A moment later, I felt him latch on, start tugging. It hurt, the area already tender and bruised, but I tried to keep that off my face.

"If you try to put anything in my mouth, I'll bite it off," I warned.

They all laughed this time, one of them, the one I guessed made the original comment, giving me a wink. "I might like that, little thrall. I can handle it if you want to take me roughly."

"Not me," another one butted in. "I like it gentle. Will you stroke me like you're stroking him, baby?"

I don't know what made me do it, wasn't aware of the impulse till my lips were curling back and the warning hiss was rolling out of my mouth. It didn't have the intended effect. Instead of being chastised, they were amused, two of them standing up and heading toward me.

"Now you're flirting," one said. He jerked his head toward Finn. "That's enough. Back away from him now." He smirked. "If you want to comfort someone, you can comfort me. The bastard cracked my ribs."

"Good," I snarled, but fear and adrenaline was making my pulse race. Finn was still drawing hard on my wrist, but I couldn't tell how much he'd taken, or how much he'd need. "Stay away from us!"

"I said time's up," he growled, his stare sharpening. "What are you doing there, anyway? Turn around so I can see."

I didn't, hunching my shoulders, hiding my wrist as long as I could.

"Run," I muttered out of the side of my mouth. "Get help."

"Move away," the Warrior said, closing the distance between us faster now. "Last warning."

"Fuck," someone shouted. "Is she . . .I think she's feeding him!"

CHAPTER SEVENTEEN

The game was up, then. The Warriors descended on us in a fury of movement, and beside me Finn exploded up from his sprawl on the ground, snapping the manacles around his wrists in one violent jerk, all pretense gone.

"Run!" I screamed at him. "Run!"

He didn't run, though. He attacked. Moving so fast my gaze could follow him only as a blur, he crashed into the closest Warrior, taking him to the ground, his face pressed into the Warrior's neck in a weirdly intimate caress. It lasted only a heartbeat, though and then he was up, launching himself at the next.

The Warrior remained laid out on the floor, staring up at the sun streaming through the trees, his throat torn and bloodied, his chest still.

By the time I'd registered that he was dead and looked toward Finn, another Warrior was down, clutching at his arm — which was no longer attached to his body. He looked as astonished as I was, though the expression was wiped from his face when Finn clamped both hands on either side of his face and twisted, snapping his neck.

He was like a tornado, biting, slicing with his claws, lashing out with kicks and punches. The Warriors had been taken unawares, but they were fighting in earnest, now. Their blows landed, I saw that, but Finn ignored them, continuing to attack like a man possessed even when his shoulder was wrenched out of its socket.

In less time that I would have thought possible, he'd

destroyed the five Warriors, their bodies limp and lifeless and strewn across the room, some of them in multiple pieces. The scent of blood was thick in the air, the sudden quiet deafening until it was pierced by a furious roar.

I had a moment to twist my head and see the Alpha pause in the doorway, rage in his eyes as he surveyed the scene, before he threw himself forward. This time Finn waited, letting the Alpha come to him. He met him with claws unsheathed and I saw them pierce the thick skin of the Alpha's sides as they tumbled backward. I scrambled to my feet, wanting to be able to see, afraid for Finn even though he'd dispatched the other five with relative ease — *because* he'd already exhausted himself fighting the other five and dislocated his shoulder in process.

I only made it a step, though, before I crashed back down to my knees, all of my strength gone. I stayed where I'd fallen, stunned, my mind somehow slow and muddled, as the fight went on across the room, its story told me to in a series of snarls and loud thumps, the shattering of glass. I tried to get up again, but the floor around me was slippery. It took longer than it should have for me to understand that was because it was slick with blood. My blood. The wound at my wrist was bleeding heavily, Finn hadn't had time to seal it.

Alarmed, I tried to stem the bleeding with my other hand, but my fingers felt thick and clumsy. My vision was sliding away, the room blackening at the edges. I had the presence of mind to scan the floor for my bandage, slapping it over the torn skin and applying pressure.

Finn, where was Finn? I weaved as I looked for him, dimly remembering he was fighting the Alpha Warrior. It was so hard to concentrate, my fear for him sliding away as a curious sleepiness stole over me. I blinked once, twice, the world taking longer to come back into focus each time.

"Finn?" I called.

A snarl came in response. I turned my head, searching for the source of the sound and saw him, covered in blood, the Alpha's head—and only the head—clutched in one hand as he crouched on a large dining table. He was covered in blood and he looked demented. I made a small sound, a whimper and his head twitched toward me lightning fast.

That was not Finn looking out at me, that was someone, or something, else.

"Help," I pleaded.

I started to fall backward, my body numb. Inwardly, I braced, waiting for the pain as my skull connected with the hard tile, but it never came. Finn was there before I hit the ground, one hand cupping the back of head, the other around my back. He lowered me gently, worried face looming over me.

"Your eyes," I mumbled, reaching a hand up to touch his face, though I lost strength halfway through. "They're yours again."

My nonsense words seemed to concern him even more than my listless body. He shook me gently, ears pinned back in distress.

"Lana? What's wrong? Tell me what's the matter."

"Too much blood." The words came out a mush. My head felt heavy, lolling back against his hold.

I felt him lift my wrist and pull the bandage free, the cool air setting off a mild sting against my skin.

"Fuck," he hissed. His tongue was warm and wet as he lapped at it, then he wrapped the bandage back into place. It was too tight, my whole hand throbbing.

"Hurts," I gasped.

"I'm sorry, Lana," he said frantically. "I'm so sorry. Here. Drink."

Drink? My paralyzed brain was too slow to work out what he meant before his wrist was pressed against my mouth, blood pooling between my lips. I gagged on it, tried to twist away, but he held me firmly.

"Take it," he insisted. "It'll help."

I didn't have the strength to resist. I swallowed, mouthful after mouthful as Finn held me in place. This wasn't like before, wasn't a taste. This was a feeding. It was bitter and viscous, the consistency of cold oil. I could feel it slide down my throat, coat my stomach. A moment later, it started to burn.

And then I burned.

Semi-conscious, I felt my whole body tingle. My heartbeat thundered through my veins, making the wound on my wrist throb until my whole arm felt like it was pulsing. Then, other places started to ache. My nipples stiffened to painful peaks and my core clenched.

"No," I mumbled, writhing. I didn't like this. Not when I was so weak I couldn't lift my head, my thoughts like treacle. I felt out of control, my body lighting up without my permission.

"It's all right," Finn whispered. "You're safe, I have you. The bleeding has stopped now." He made an unhappy noise. "Little one, I've covered you in their blood. Hang on, I'm going to get us somewhere where we can wash it off."

He picked me up, and then we were moving. My vision was still foggy, the rooms passing by in a blur that made me nauseous. Closing my eyes, I let darkness consume me, the heat from Finn's blood washing over me in red waves. It was a strange mix of pleasure and pain, riding the razor edge, never letting me roll into ecstasy or feel the whip of agony.

I floated, more out of my body than in, paying no attention to where Finn took me. I trusted him to look after me. I wasn't aware of him closing us in a bathroom, or of him removing my clothes, using claws to slice them off my body, but I came back to myself with a rush when he stepped with me into the warm water of a shower, droplets cascading down onto my oversensitive skin.

I gasped, eyes flying open, struggling in his grasp, but he tightened his hold, soothing me with his voice.

"Lana, it's okay. It's me. It's just me. You're safe."

"Put me down," I begged.

"You'll fall."

"I won't. I—please. Put me down."

Reluctantly, Finn lowered my feet to the floor, keeping his tight grip on me, expecting my legs to fold beneath me. They didn't. I felt strong. Supercharged. My every muscle sung, my body practically vibrating with life.

"Are you all right?" he asked, his expression concerned.

"I feel good," I told him. "I feel amazing." I turned into him, realizing suddenly that he was as naked as I was. "Are you all right? Your shoulder—" I ran my hand up his chest and over the shoulder in question. It felt all right to my untutored hands, but I had seen it twist to an impossible angle, heard the joint pop.

"I put it back in," he told me gruffly.

"Will it heal? Do you need—"

His glower stoppered my mouth. "If you dare offer me your blood after what just happened—"

After what just happened. The images replayed themselves over in my head, but they had a shadowy, filmy quality to them, like a television show that I'd watched half asleep, or after several glasses of wine. One thing stood out though. Those eyes, staring out of Finn's face.

"What did my blood do to you?" I asked hesitantly, the water cascading down my face and tangling in my eyelashes as I looked up at him. "It didn't just make you stronger. You were . . .changed."

Finn froze, going preternaturally still. I thought I saw a flash of the same strangeness in his eyes, but when he blinked it was gone again.

"It unleashed my dragon," he said quietly. "I couldn't transform, but my beast was going crazed, knowing you were in danger. When you fed it your blood, it filled up my skin, gave me its strength. That was why I was able to—" He shrugged, grimacing.

"Tear them into pieces," I finished for him.

"I frightened you," Finn said regretfully. He lifted a hand to touch my face then thought better of it.

"You saved me," I told him, taking the hand and holding it to my chest, my heart. "I thought you'd run, get help—"

"And leave you there alone?"

"I'd have survived," I said, a lot braver now that it was all over. "I knew you'd come back and save me."

"Hmmm." He pressed his lips together, the hesitant, apologetic Finn disappearing and being replaced by one who looked a lot less impressed with me. "You expected me to abandon you, to run away and save myself. Leave you, my mate, there alone with six Warriors?"

With every word he took a step closer, until he was hemming me in against the wall, the cascade of the shower falling on him now.

"Yes?" I offered.

His eyes narrowed further. "Six Warriors who not only wanted to take you as their thrall, but who wanted to mate with you?" He paused, leaning down until his face was just above mine. "And you thought I should run?"

"I thought they were going to kill you," I protested.

He made a deep rumble in his chest, then he dipped down, slid both hands around the back of my thighs and hoisted me up so we were face to face, eye to eye, my legs spread around his hips.

"Neither myself nor my dragon are very pleased with you right now," he growled.

It shouldn't have been arousing, *I* shouldn't be aroused,

not when the Warriors' blood was still being sluiced off Finn's skin by the shower, but the position we were in put my pussy right over Finn's very erect cock, and all of my erogenous zones were still engorged and tingling from the rush of his blood. I hadn't come then, too afraid and disoriented, too shocked, but I wanted to now.

"Maybe I can make it up to you?" I offered, wiggling slightly. He didn't take the bait.

"Which reminds me," he went on, as if I hadn't spoken, "that you are also in trouble for the way you behaved at the lake."

"At the lake?" I asked, confused. "What did I do?"

"I told you to stay put, but I distinctly saw you coming toward me, toward danger."

Oh. Yes. I did do that. "I listened the second time."

"The second time," he repeated.

"I'm sorry?" I offered. When he didn't look appeased, I lifted myself a little higher, my body performing the move almost effortlessly thanks to Finn's transfusion, and placed a soft kiss on his lips. "Very sorry."

"You know," he said conversationally, all the while beginning a slow, *slow*, glide of his cock along my pussy. "I had a seduction all planned out at the lake." He paused, pupils narrowing to slits. "You would have enjoyed it."

I quirked a small smile, tilting my pelvis in the hopes that he'd grind into me a little harder. "We're still in the water," I pointed out.

"Hmmm," he agreed. "Only now you're in trouble."

I opened my mouth to apologize again, arousal tempered with a hint of wariness now, but I never got the chance. He moved suddenly, slipping his arms beneath my legs and hoisting my knees higher. Then he surged inside. I gasped, all the air leaving my lungs. He was deep, impossibly deep. My balance was precarious, entirely dependent on his hold on my legs. I couldn't move, could only hover there, motionless, as he pulled back and then thrust forward even harder.

It was bliss, my clit already twitching with the need to come, the water warm and running in soothing rivulets over my skin. I closed my eyes and leaned back, enjoying it, when a loud smack rang out. I felt the sharp sting a moment later, blooming across my right buttock.

Eyes flying open, I stared into the gaze of the dragon.

"You won't tell me to leave you ever again," he commanded.

Thrust and retreat. Thrust and retreat.

Smack.

"You will listen when I give you an order for your safety."

I was panting, torn between the pleasure of his slow, deep thrusts and the sting of his hand on my backside and helplessly turned on by the authority in his voice, the dominance of the dragon.

"Yes?" he asked. I didn't reply quickly enough and he spanked me again.

That was it, that was the word. He was *spanking* me. I'd never been spanked, not even as a child. I'd never understood how it could be erotic. I did now.

"Yes, Lana?"

I nodded, too lost in the rush of my upcoming orgasm to form words.

Smack!

"Say it!"

"Yes!" I cried the word as I came, my back arching, toes curling as it ran up my body, stealing my breath. "Oh God, Finn! God!"

I might have come, but he hadn't. Pressing me tighter against the wall, he started to hammer into me. It was too fast, too deep, my tissues too sensitive. I squirmed, trying to get away from the rawness of it, but I was trapped. Forced to accept it, I drew in a shuddering breath as a second orgasm ripped through me, this one making my muscles tremble and jerk against Finn as he finally stilled, buried deep, and released inside me.

"Mate," he murmured. "*My* mate. Mine."

It was the dragon and it was him. One and the same. I lifted my hand and cupped the back of his head, holding him to me as he squeezed me tight.

"Yours," I agreed. "All of yours."

CHAPTER EIGHTEEN

She wasn't at the den. Vall's dragon roared in agitation as it stood, took up the full space of the landing pad and peered in through the windows. It didn't matter that it couldn't see anything beyond the living room, it could *sense* it.

Not there.

Where was she? Where the fuck was she?

Launching up into the sky again, it began hunting. Half a beast, half a man, its thoughts flitted back and forth between intelligent rationale and primal instinct. The more civilized side was allowed to make suggestions, guide the search, the dragon took sole responsibility for hunting.

Not in the valley, not out on the plains. Not in at the lake, although . . .

Something glinted, out of place and the dragon swooped down to investigate. Landing with a thump on the sandy shoreline, it tilted its enormous head and sniffed at the mangled remains of the skimmer. Finn's. Covered in Finn-scent. Also Lana-scent. And food.

But they weren't there.

There was blood, though. The blood of strangers, male strangers, and that incited the rage inside the dragon even further. Finn-blood, too. Freshly spilled. The dragon prowled, its gaze making one more sweep, when it paused. Growled. Sniffed the air hard.

There. Just a drop, on a sandy area disturbed in a pattern the man-thoughts said was caused by a hover vehicle. The scent of the strangers and Lana. Lana and fear.

Bellowing in outrage, the dragon thrust upward, wings beating hard, neck strained toward the sky. It had a new prey now. Bad prey. Saliva pooled in its jaws as it imagined bones crunching, flesh meat.

The scent of the strangers was dimly familiar. A place whispered in the back of its mind, a thread of memory that guided him to a location, deep in the trees.

He smelled the blood from a long way away. It got stronger as he swooped lower until it was all he could smell. Blood and death. The scent of Lana's blood was faint in comparison, but it was the scent of his mate, he would never miss it. She'd bled there.

Infuriated, he landed on the roof, crashing through the glass. The space was small and he couldn't find Lana as the beast, so he folded back into the smaller shape, letting the more civilized mind come forward. Find her, it urged. Hunt our mate.

Vall's eyes flicked from side to side as he took in the utter devastation of the room. Dead bodies were scattered across the floor, draped over furniture. There were limbs detached from bodies, a head, lolling on its own. Blood saturated the furnishings, sprayed up the wall. An almighty battle had been fought here.

He crossed the room silently, although the dragon had announced their arrival in emphatic style, shattering the glass skylights. There was no sign of Finn or Lana, though there was a sizable pool of Lana's blood spread across one section of tile and Finn's scent was strong there also.

"Lana!" The sight of so much red, more blood, it seemed than she could possibly have in her body, broke Vall's military training that told him to proceed in silence, be a stealthy predator. If she was here, if she was hurt, he had to find her.

"Vall?" It was Finn, not Lana who called in response. He followed the direction of the shout and found them dressing in a small bathroom, Lana pulling on clothes that weren't hers. The scent of sex was fresh and strong and Finn had a relaxed, satisfied air about him at odds with the carnage in the other room.

"What the fuck happened?" Vall demanded. He couldn't wait for an answer, he crossed the room and dragged Lana into his arms, both halves of him needing to know that she was whole and well, feel her heartbeat beneath her skin.

"We were ambushed at the lake," Finn replied. He'd lost his relaxed look, was hunching his shoulders defensively. "It was in the middle of our territory, it should have been safe."

With great difficulty, Vall stopped himself from berating his Second for removing Lana from the safety of the den. He was right, the lake was deep in their territory, he wouldn't have hesitated to take Lana there himself.

"You think it was planned?"

Finn nodded. "They knew about her stars."

Vall tensed, everything in him coming to a sudden stop. "How could they have?"

"Danin and Bern?" Finn suggested. "They were the only other ones who knew."

Even though Finn's words made sense, Vall couldn't believe it. "They wouldn't," he said. "I trust them absolutely."

"Maybe it was just luck," Finn offered, though Vall could see he didn't believe it. "Maybe they came across the entry in the database."

Vall shook his head. "If Danin said he'd bury it, he buried it. The chances of someone stumbling across it accidentally are non-existent."

"Well, they found out somehow," Finn said, his expression unhappy.

Vall shrugged. Putting the mystery aside for now, he turned to more important matters, his mate.

"Are you all right?" he murmured. She'd cuddled into him

as soon as he'd gathered her in his arms, and now she kept her face down, her head pressed into his chest. "Lana?"

He felt her nod, heard a small, muffled, "Yes."

"Look at me then," he coaxed.

He waited, the moment drawing out, then she whispered, "I can't."

What? Ice formed in his veins, his heart stuttering in his chest. She was afraid to look at him? He turned to Finn, the dragon within him preparing to storm back through to the blood-soaked living area and kill the bastards all over again.

"What did they do to her?" he asked, voice low and deadly.

"Nothing," Finn said, frowning. "They didn't hurt her. Right, Lana?" He paused, eyes widening in sudden horror. "Did *I* hurt you?"

"No." She shook her head, but she still wouldn't look up.

"What is it? What's wrong?" Vall asked, getting desperate.

"I don't know," she said. "I just can't."

Taking a firm grip of her upper arms and shifting her away from him, Vall crooked a finger and tucked it under her chin, forcing her face up. She resisted at first and when she eventually gave in, she kept her gaze downcast.

"Lana," he pleaded. "Look at me."

The dragon understood before he did. It had been shifting inside him, sensing something . . .not wrong, but different. But then it had Lana in its arms and it was a simple creature, it didn't question beyond that. When she finally flashed her gaze up to meet his, it was a punch in the gut. Time stopped and he could do nothing but stare at her.

It was Finn's exclamation that brought him back to himself.

"Lana!" he second gasped. "What — ?"

She dropped her gaze again, tried to worm her way back into Vall's side, but he held her back.

"Let me see," he murmured.

Reluctantly, she met his gaze and held it. Her pupils

contracted in the light, the slit tightening until it was a thin line down the center of her eye. The iris, which had been a beautiful rich brown before, now shone a glittering gold.

"Can you see it?" she asked. "I feel it in me."

"I see it," Vall said.

"I didn't know what it was until you arrived," she confessed shyly. She pushed to come back to him and this time he let her. "I just thought I was feeling funny because of Finn's blood." Finn's blood? Vall raised a questioning eyebrow at his Second, but then he remembered the pool of Lana's blood in the living area. If his Second had fed her, he'd likely saved her life. Vall would have done the same. "But now that you're here . . ." Lana tailed off, tucking her shoulders in as she sought to get even closer to him.

Now that she'd met the pack Alpha. That was what she was feeling, the need to submit to him, to show that she understood his dominance.

It wouldn't always be like this, but the dragon had only just awoken in her, was immediately faced with its new Alpha and his Second. Of course that would be intimidating.

"It's all right," Vall said gently. "She just needs a moment to settle. To understand that she's ours and we're not going to hurt her."

"Is this supposed to happen?" Lana asked, daring a bashful glance up at him.

In a word? No. Females did not carry the dragon inside them. Vall exchanged a glance with Finn and his Second shook his head. He'd never heard of it either. But then, Lana wasn't Triniun and she was a seven-star female. They had no idea what she could do.

"We'll ask Danin and Bern to look into it," he promised.

"And we can ask them whether they've run their mouths off about our seven-star female," Finn muttered darkly.

Vall nodded, though he knew what the answer would be.

How the Warriors had found out about Lana was a question for another day, however. He wanted her out of there, back to the den. He wanted her dragon home, surrounded by her pack.

"How did you find us," Lana asked suddenly. "How did you know we were here?"

"I tracked you," Vall said. "I sensed you were in trouble and I flew to the den, but you weren't there." The panic of that discovery still thrummed through his veins. He doubted he'd let her out of his sight for a season. "I found the remains of the skimmer at the lake and I recognized one of the Warriors' scents. I don't know them, not well, but I knew they denned here."

There was a heavily silent pause, then Finn said quietly, "You flew?"

He met his Second's gaze, adrenaline flushing through him as the dragon swelled with triumph in his chest. "I transformed," he said. "Fully. When I realized Lana was in danger, it gave me the strength to bring the beast forth."

"You became the dragon?" Finn whispered, astonished.

"I did."

"But how did you know that I needed you?" Lana asked. "What do you mean, you sensed I was in danger?"

"I don't understand it," Vall admitted, "and I've never heard of it happening before, but we have a blood bond, you and I. And now, you and Finn. That creates a strong connection. Somehow, my dragon felt your fear."

"Incredible," Finn said, shaking his head in awe.

It was. No, Vall corrected himself. *She* was. Lana was the incredible one. He'd been right, she was going to change all their lives. Change their entire world.

They were walking to the garage, Lana close by his side, one of her hands tightly wrapped around his and her gaze studiously focused away from the grisly scene in the living area, when she suddenly paused.

"Where's their thrall?" she asked.

"What?"

"The Alpha Warrior, he said he was going to swap their thrall for yours. So where is she?"

Good question. She was probably hiding somewhere, too scared to come out. Or, perhaps, she was locked in and couldn't. Though he wanted nothing more than to get out of there, Vall wouldn't leave a terrified female to face the remains of the battle alone.

Exchanging a look with Finn, he motioned to Lana to stay where she was, then began trying the doors along the hallway. They were all empty, mostly just untidy bedrooms or storerooms, but one was locked. It was a thick, sturdy door. When Vall put his head to it, he could hear nothing inside. He knocked, listening hard and heard a small intake in breath.

"She's in here," he said.

Finn and Lana joined him at the door, Finn sliding an arm around Lana and drawing her back slightly as Vall put a shoulder to the door and slammed against it. It didn't budge, but the person on the other side gave another shocked little gasp, this one more of a whimper.

"Are you in there?" Vall called. "You're safe, we're not going to hurt you. Can you open the door?"

No answer. He shoved at it again, but it refused to give way.

On the other side of the door, the thrall was now quietly crying.

"Hello?" Lana stepped forward, pressing her hand to the door's surface. "Are you in there? Don't be afraid, I promise they won't hurt you. They're going to get you out." She paused, looked back toward the living area where the pack lay in pieces. "We're going to take you away from here."

The crying stopped and soft, shuffling footsteps

approached the door.

"I can't get out," a small voice replied. "The door is handprinted."

Vall had seen the discreet little security panel beside the door. He pressed his hand to it now but it gave an angry little beep, flashing red twice.

"I could go and get the Alpha's hand?" Finn suggested.

Lana wrinkled her nose, horrified at the idea, but Vall shook his head. "Needs to be warm," he said. "It'll register that he's got no pulse. We'll need to force it, come and help me."

Even with the two of them working together, it took several attempts before the reinforced door collapsed under their assault. When they fell inside the room, the thrall had retreated to the furthest corner, huddled on the bed with her legs drawn up under her. She looked terrified, bruises decorating her face. Making an unwelcome pattern down the length of both arms were bite marks—the Warriors hadn't bothered to clean or heal the wounds where they'd fed. Even if the pack hadn't taken Lana, Vall would have wanted to kill them for this alone.

Lana made a shocked noise behind him and he turned to see her standing in the doorway. Her gaze was fixed on the thrall.

"I know you!" she said. "You were at the challenges!"

CHAPTER NINETEEN

I couldn't take my gaze off the poor woman sitting opposite me in the hover vehicle. It wasn't ours, we'd stolen the Warrior pack's transport. They weren't exactly going to need it anymore. Their thrall, whose name I discovered was Mina, had tucked herself into a seat as far from Vall and Finn as possible, staying small and motionless, as if she were trying to be invisible.

Though she hadn't been covered in bruises and bite marks the last time I'd seen her, her face had been just as wretched. She was the unhappy woman who'd stood beside me as we watched the fights, had been picked third to last, rejected because she didn't have any stars.

It could have been me. That was the thought running on a constant loop in my head. The Warrior had stood there, angry at his performance and scowled at us both, unimpressed with the selection left to him. He could so easily have taken me instead of Mina. I felt incredibly sorry for her, but I was also massively relieved. And I felt bad about that, too.

"Where are you taking her?" I asked Vall, because I was sure Mina would want to know but I was also certain that she was too afraid to speak.

"We're going home," Vall said. "I'll get Lyne to take her into the city. We'll hand her over to an Administrator and they can work out what to do with her."

Mina didn't look very happy with that, but she nodded anyway.

"I want to go home," she said, her voice a rasp, probably

because of the multi-colored marks encircling her throat. Her face screwed up with tears. "But I can't. I can't ever go back. They'd be so ashamed that I . . .that I failed."

I bit my lip as she leaned forward, propped her head onto her knees and started crying in earnest. I wanted to comfort her, but she didn't know me at all. We'd spent a traumatic couple of hours in each other's company, but had spoken only a handful of words.

"Her family should never have sent her here," Finn muttered, looking back at the thrall from the controls with a frown. "No marks. She was always going to have a hell of a time."

"Why would they?" I asked.

"Money?" Vall offered. "It's a five-year service, and it's well paid. The thrall's living expenses are covered, so it's all money in the hand."

"That's awful!"

He shrugged. "Most are volunteers. They might be living in poverty, or have no prospects where they are. Five years of being looked after, then retired with honor and a good pension is seen by a lot of women as a good deal."

"Did she look like she was being looked after?" I asked Vall angrily.

The weird shyness that had come over me before was slowly seeping away. The new, strange feeling in my chest wasn't, though. The dragon. It was a bizarre idea, but I couldn't come up with any other explanation for what I felt, and then Vall had shown me my face in a mirror before we'd left the bathroom. Or more specifically, my eyes.

They'd been normal, unassuming human eyes. A nice shade of brown that made me think of chocolate—although to be fair, quite a lot of things made me think of chocolate. Not anymore. In the mirror, the first thing to shock me was the gleaming gold staring back at me. That had been startling enough, but what was really alien about my transformation was the fact my pupils had shifted from little round dots to convex slits. I couldn't decide if they were creepy or cool, but they were definitely different.

I'd thought I'd felt something strange inside me before, something Other. The sips I'd had from Vall must have triggered something. When Finn gave me a much bigger transfusion of blood, it completed the process. If I was honest, I thought it was incredible, but also absolutely terrifying and I was on board with Vall's plan to get his Thinker friends Danin and Bern to examine my blood as soon as possible, to find out what was really going on.

When we got back to the den, the pack's hover vehicle was already on the landing pad, parked haphazardly as if whoever had been driving it had been in a hurry. The doors were open and as Finn touched the second hover down, Jay and Lyne came bursting back outside.

"Is she there? Do you have her?" Jay demanded.

"Is she all right?" Lyne grabbed at the edge of the hover, anxiety written all over his face.

"I'm okay," I said, drawing both Warriors' attention.

There was a silent pause while they looked at me, searching for injury and finding changes instead.

"Your eyes," Jay breathed.

"We don't know what's going on," I explained. "It happened after Finn had to feed me."

"Finn had to *feed* you?" Jay squawked.

"Let's go inside," Vall ordered. "We'll explain everything. Lyne, go and contact Danin and Bern. Tell them I want them here now. If they argue, you can tell them I brought forth my dragon."

We headed inside and the three of us brought Jay and Lyne up to speed. Lyne took Mina down to the city in the dead pack's hover vehicle. I could see that he didn't want to leave, could almost feel his dragon's reluctance to leave mine, but being surrounded by four strange Warriors after her ordeal was too much for Mina. She was shaking, her skin waxen and cold to the touch.

"That could so easily have been me," I repeated what I'd been thinking earlier, listening to the sound of the hover's engine rev as Lyne guided it off the platform. "The Alpha Warrior stood there, choosing between the two of us." I glanced at my Warriors, who were hovering around me like a pack of nannies after my ordeal. "It could have been me."

Vall dismissed my truth with a shake of his head. "They would never have treated you the way they did her," he said. "All it would have taken was one sip of your blood for them to know what they had in their hands. They would have cherished you."

Maybe, but I doubted the other pack's version of cherished would have matched mine. "All the same, I'm glad I'm here," I told him.

They liked that, Vall especially. His eyes glowed quicksilver bright as the dragon came to the fore to preen at me.

"I feel him," I whispered, astonished. "I feel your dragon reaching for me."

"You're our mate," he said simply. Then his gaze, too, went toward the door and the landing pad beyond, the hover vehicle that was already far out of sight. "I still don't understand how they knew about you."

"I should have left one alive," Finn said unhappily. "We could have interrogated them. I lost control and let the dragon take over. It wasn't interested in anything other than bathing in their blood."

I blanched, remembering Finn standing there, coated in the remains of the other pack. He wasn't exaggerating, he'd literally ripped them to bits with his teeth and claws. He'd been the dragon, even if he'd still worn his more human-looking shape.

"What about Rin?" I suggested.

"Who?" Vall asked. "The Administrator?"

I shrugged. "He knew I wasn't normal." I remembered back to that day. Vall had been furious to be late and disgusted to be left with me, the left over, unmarked female. Then he'd taken one sip of my blood and swept me out of there with nary another word. Strange behavior. "He saw your reaction—he might have looked me up later to see if you'd had me tested."

"Danin buried that record," Jay said.

"Yes," I agreed, "but if he was looking for me specifically, I bet he could find it."

"Administrators are trained to know the ins and outs of all our systems," Finn murmured. "It wouldn't have been that hard."

"Though why tell that pack?" I wondered.

Jay shrugged. "Maybe they were friends? It could be as simple as that."

"That would be easy enough to find out," Vall said. He looked to Finn. "When did Danin and Bern say they'd be here?"

"Soon." He frowned. "They said they were already on their way. That they had news."

"Good."

While we waited for the two Thinkers to arrive, Jay, Finn and Vall pampered me, fussing over the water in my bath, hand feeding me a meal and stroking and petting me any time I wandered within reach. I could feel the agitation still rolling off them in waves, so I endured the coddling with good grace, though I was relieved when my ears, thankfully the same shape but now with much sharper hearing, picked up the rumble of a vehicle approaching.

I wasn't allowed to go out onto the platform and greet

Danin and Bern, so I had to wait behind Jay's protective bulk as Vall and Finn went outside and frisked them for weapons, shined a light in their eyes to check for nefarious intentions. Probably not, but they were taking protection of me to a new level, deliberately keeping their bodies — all their bodies — in between me and Danin and Bern at all times.

"You said you had news," Vall said, getting straight to the point. "We do as well. I need you to test Lana's blood again and mine. See what's changed." He paused. "Do you have what you need with you? I won't take Lana out of the den until Lyne is back and only if we need to."

"I have what we'll need," Danin promised, a large carrycase in one hand and his tablet in the other. Bern, too, was laden with equipment. They dropped them on the dining room table and then approached me, coming as close as Vall, Finn and Jay would let them.

I saw it the moment they registered the differences in me. Danin's mouth fell open and Bern actually swayed as if he might faint.

"You are evolving," Danin gasped. He took an eager step forward. "I have to take a sample."

He was stopped short by Finn, who stepped into his path.

"This is our mate," he growled. "She's not a science experiment, you'll treat her with respect."

"Of course," Danin barked, frowning and trying to get around Finn. When the Warrior simply stepped with him, Danin paused and looked up into Finn's face. Whatever he saw there made him hesitate a moment, his expression losing its avarice. "Of course," he repeated, much more solemnly.

Once Finn felt sure he'd made his point, he moved aside and Danin approached me, cautiously this time.

"May I take a sample?" he asked, deliberately courteous.

Silently, I held out my arm, let him draw some of my blood with his little machine.

"Take a sample from me as well," Vall instructed. "I am changed also."

"How so?" Danin asked, pausing halfway back to Bern and his equipment, my blood sample clenched in his hand.

"I called the dragon. Fully shifted. I don't know that I could do it again, call it at will, but it's awakened within me."

Danin looked like all his Christmases had come at once. He practically threw my sample at Bern in his haste to get over to Vall and pull blood out of him.

"You said you had news," Vall commented as Danin took the sample. "What is it?"

Danin snorted. "I was coming to tell you that I'd detected changes in your blood. That your testosterone had gone off the charts and that your cells were reacting strangely. It seems you found out for yourself."

He took the second sample over to Bern, who had set up something of a mini laboratory on the dining room table and already had my blood under the microscope. Jay, Finn and I edged closer, watching as Bern worked.

"Look," he muttered to Danin. "Look! The markers we saw before are much more pronounced. If I didn't know better, I'd think this sample came from a full Triniun female."

"I took some of Finn's blood," I volunteered. "Could that be why?"

Bern was too busy looking at my strange results to lift his head, but Danin answered for him.

"No," he said. "Your body would process that, almost like food. You might draw strength from it, but it would be a temporary thing. It should not have entered your bloodstream."

"It has," Bern contradicted. "Here." He held out a hand to Danin. "Give me Vall's sample."

Danin handed it over and Bern used a dropper to extract a small amount and add it to the smear of my blood on the little glass slide. He immediately thrust his face back down to stare through the lens and drew in a sharp, astonished breath. "Danin!" he called.

Danin almost threw his partner out of the way to get to the microscope. It would have been funny if it hadn't been my sample they were looking at, my strangely changing blood that was causing such a stir.

"It's as if her blood is absorbing elements from our DNA." Danin breathed deeply. "She's like a natural sponge, pulling in things that make her stronger."

"But look at Vall's sample," Bern said, gaze fixed down the lens of a second microscope he'd unearthed from somewhere. "The reactions we saw before have increased exponentially."

They continued to mutter back and forth, using words I didn't understand, their excitement palpable. Glancing over at Vall, Finn and Jay, I could see they were just as lost as I was.

"Danin!" Vall barked, tired of waiting. "What do you see? Be sure to use words us lowly Warriors can understand." His tone was more threat than joke.

Though he looked like the last thing he wanted to do was leave whatever amazing things were unfolding beneath his microscope, Danin stepped away from the table.

"Lana's blood is changing," he said. "She is becoming more like us. Triniun. There are markers in her blood that we normally only see in Warriors who are strong with the dragon."

"I might be able to shift into a dragon?" I squeaked. I wasn't sure if I loved that idea or was terrified by it. A bit of both, I thought.

"No woman has ever been able to transform," Danin cautioned. "Not even in our history."

"But?" Vall pressed.

"I can guarantee nothing, but the changes we've seen so far are pronounced. It may be possible."

"And my blood?"

Danin faced Vall head on, his excitement barely held in

check. "Your blood is more like what I would expect to see if you could somehow go back in time, catch me a dragon and bring it back here for me to test. You were right, Vall. You are fully awakened."

"I'm not sure that I could shift now," Vall cautioned. "The dragon is there, but it's —"

"Resting? How many feeds have you taken from your mate?"

"Full feeds? One."

"And yet already you have managed to transform. There are no guarantees, but I'd be willing to bet at least Bern's right arm that you could do it again." He quirked a hairless brow. "And I have a lot of use for that arm."

Really? I tried to bite back my smirk when Bern grumbled, "Danin!" When Vall had said they were partners, I hadn't realized they were *partners*.

"Your mate is extraordinary," Danin finished. "There are none like her in all of Trinia, she is utterly unique."

"Every Warrior on the planet is going to want her," Jay spat. "How the hell are we supposed to keep her safe?"

Vall turned to look at me, his expression shrewd. I could see what he was thinking, knew what was going to come out of his mouth before he said it.

"We keep her here, out of sight."

"No," I said. Locked up, like the other thrall had been? "I don't want to live like that!"

Danin, too, looked unconvinced. "We've been over this. You cannot keep her existence a secret."

"Why not?" Vall challenged.

"Because the secret is already out!" he exclaimed. "Finn told us what happened, how she was kidnapped. Those Warriors were not acting alone."

"So we find who sent them and shut them up too."

"You presume they have not told anyone," Danin argued

flatly. "That they have left no evidence of what they know. And how will you explain the demise of a full pack? What reason will you give for why you had to put them down?"

"There's the other thrall too," I added, very much on Danin's side. "She knows about me and she saw my face. She knows how many stars I have."

Vall set his face mulishly. "I can call Lyne back, he will not have reached the city yet. The thrall can be quietly dealt with."

"Vall, no!" My words came out sharply, but also resonant with something else, something deeper. My dragon, I realized. She was speaking with me. "I won't be your mate if that's how you act," I said and meant it.

It made sense to Vall, I could see that. It was neat and clean and it got him what he wanted, me, here with him and the pack. Safe and sound.

"There's no other way," he growled, but his look was pleading.

"Go to the Sovereign," Bern suggested in a low voice. We all turned to look at him, and it was only then that he lifted his gaze from his work, looking slightly uncomfortable at the sudden attention. "That's the best way to get what you want," he said.

"How do you figure?" Jay asked.

"You won't be able to keep this quiet," he said, gaze on Vall. "No matter how many people you kill. Your only option is to reveal her to the public, declare her your pack mate. Better yet, have her declare that she has chosen your pack to mate." He glanced at me quickly, then away again. "You have *dragons* in your pack, Vall. Do you understand what that means? It elevates you higher than any other Warrior in Trinia. It elevates you higher than the Sovereign!"

"He isn't a Warrior," Finn said.

"He isn't a Thinker, either," Danin replied drolly. "The

Administrators had him declared one because the only other option was Idiot. But the Sovereign has not always been a Thinker. Back before our race lost the ability to shift, it was *never* anything but a Warrior." He paused. "According to precedence, you should rule."

The room fell silent as we all digested that. I turned toward Vall, who was looking distinctly uncomfortable.

"You should be king?" I asked jokingly. "Do you get a crown?"

"I don't want to rule," Vall replied quickly. He looked hard at Bern. "I don't."

Bern shrugged. "Well, you'll have to convince the Sovereign of that. But if the people know you have the power to shift, that you are the dragon, you will be as safe as you can be. Mates are sacrosanct, and the mate who brought our greatest gift back to our people? No one could take Lana from you without huge uproar."

Vall didn't like it, his face folding into a scowl, but looking around the room I could see it made sense to everyone else.

"You will come to the city with us?" he demanded, looking from Danin to Bern. "Explain to the Sovereign what you have discovered in your experiments?"

Both Thinkers looked unhappy now, but Danin gave a nod. "We will."

"Use small words," Jay suggested dryly.

CHAPTER TWENTY

The city—finally I was getting to see it. We were travelling in two separate hover vehicles, me, Jay and Lyne in front, with Finn, Danin and Bern travelling behind. Neither Finn nor Danin and Bern had been happy about the travelling arrangements, but I was fairly sure Vall had done it to ensure the two Thinkers didn't try to abscond on the way to the palace. They didn't look enthused to be going to visit the king— or Sovereign, as they called him—and their reluctance was fueling my own.

Vall, after another small feeding from me, had shifted into the dragon, an enormous thing with wings and glittering scales and everything. It was the most astonishing thing I'd ever seen—and I'd seen a lot of astonishing things lately. He was flying in the sky high above us. He hadn't wanted to do that, had wanted to ride in the hover vehicle with me, but Danin and Bern insisted. They wanted him to be seen entering the city. They wanted there to be no way the Sovereign could get away with killing us all to try and hush things up.

After all, Vall had been considering that option himself just a short while ago.

I kept glancing up at him, gliding across the blazing blue sky. He was enormous, the size of a small plane, and his tail swished lazily as it trailed the air currents behind him, wings barely moving as he kept pace with us. When he'd changed and first launched himself up into the sky, my heart had been in my mouth, but I'd also felt a real longing to go with him. Dragon rider—there was a thought.

The idea I might be able to shift one day, as Danin had

hypothesized, was a step too far for my mind to contemplate right now.

"Here we go," Jay murmured.

I dragged my focus away from Vall's dragon to look ahead. The city, which had been a vague blur on the horizon, was now front and center. We were here.

The outer suburbs were sprawling, the houses built on large lots. They were single story and built for extreme heat, adobe-style. As we moved closer into the city center, things became more tightly packed. There were still residential areas, small blocks of flats no higher than four floors, heavy overhangs protecting the windows from the light that felt almost as intense as it did out on the plains, but there were also industrial districts and shopping centers. Honestly, it looked a lot like cities back home. The only difference was the people.

I'd been on this planet a few days now, enough to get acclimatized to the idea that I was in a different world and to come to terms with the fact I'd been picked as a thrall for a group of Warriors who drank blood to feed their beasts. But I'd been kept away from crowds and now, seeing strange faces, *alien* faces, all around me, it was really hitting home that I had to make a life here.

I couldn't deal with that on top of my upcoming visit with Triniun royalty, so I closed my eyes briefly and then focused them ahead. It was fairly obvious that we were getting close to the palace. There was a large open square with fountains dotted around it, people lazing about and enjoying the mixture of water and sun. Beyond that was an enormous building which looked almost Middle Eastern in design, like the Taj Mahal. It was the color of sand, glass colored inlays twinkling in the light. There was a central bulbous roof with lower, flatter wings separating off from it to the left and right. We coasted around the square and then parked right out front.

I gathered from the way two guards came running down

the wide white marble steps that we weren't supposed to do that.

"No!" one of them shouted, waving his arms at us. "What are you doing?"

Finn jumped out of the second hover vehicle and strode over to us, meeting the guard before he could come within ten steps of me.

"We need to see the Sovereign," he said bluntly.

The guard's face dropped in astonishment, then he laughed. "Who do you think you are? You don't just drive up and demand to see our royal leader. Get out of here."

A shadow cast over the guard's face, despite the fact it was a cloudless day and he was standing in direct sunlight. I looked up just in time to see Vall swooping in to land, his body much larger than the hover vehicle. It was much heavier, too. When he crashed down onto the steps, just feet away from the guard, the stone shattered beneath his clawed feet.

The guard's expression was comical. His mouth opened but no sound came out.

"We want to see the Sovereign," Finn repeated.

"Wait here," the guard spluttered, then when Vall gave a huff that sounded suspiciously like a growl, he added, "Please."

He turned and ran up the steps as fast as his legs could carry him, stumbling twice where the shockwaves of Vall's landing had dislodged random steps all the way to the top.

"Don't change back yet," Finn murmured, looking at the door where both guards had now disappeared. "We want you to be seen, remember?"

Vall snorted disdainfully but held onto his shape.

"I think it's fair to say he's been seen," I murmured, turning to look at the square.

We'd drawn a crowd, the lucky few who'd been present when Vall appeared moving as close as they dared, more pouring in from the streets beyond. News travelled fast, apparently.

Feeling uncomfortable with all the attention we were gathering—though it wasn't me they were looking at, at least—I clambered out of the hover vehicle and moved to stand by Vall. His hulking profile created shade from the heat of the sun, and when I put a handout to touch his shoulder—which was as high up as I could reach—his skin was cool to the touch.

"Are you all right?" I asked.

It was a stupid question—he couldn't even answer me—but it was obvious from the tense, slightly hunched way he was standing that he didn't like being so on display.

"I can't blame them for looking at you," I said. "You're magnificent."

He liked that, swinging his long neck around to give me a nuzzle that almost sent me sprawling. He made a strange grating sound then, a sort of convulsion. It took me a moment to realize he was laughing.

"Vall," Finn murmured. "The High Defender."

We both turned to look as an elderly man emerged from the palace, three Warriors following a respectful distance behind. They all looked astounded, though the High Defender had an enormous grin on his face.

"Well," he said as he reached us. "Well, well, well. Fuck me."

I spluttered, not expecting language like that from someone with a title as exulted as High Defender, and he turned to me.

"This must be your thrall, Lana."

"Our mate," Finn corrected.

The High Defender didn't look insulted by the sharpness of Finn's tone. He inclined his head in acknowledgement. "Congratulations." He frowned as he took a closer look at me.

I could practically see him counting the stars on my face. "Seven?" he asked, aghast. "Seven stars?"

He seemed more surprised by my markings than he did about the fact there was a hulking great dragon hanging out on the palace steps.

"I think you need to come inside," he said, finally serious. "We have much to discuss." He threw an amused look at Vall. "Can you transform? I don't believe you'll fit through the front doors like that." It took a moment, but Vall began to shrink, a weird process that looked like a balloon with a small puncture on a time-lapse camera. Eventually he stood there, normal sized and stark naked. The High Defender raised his brow. "And put some clothes on, the Sovereign is going to have an inferiority complex enough without having to look at that." He waved at Vall's cock, which even flaccid was impressive in its length.

Vall unearthed a pair of trousers from the hover vehicle and we headed inside the palace. The guards had returned to their post at the front door and they gaped at us as we walked past. Jay paused just behind me, turning to snap his teeth at the guard who'd berated us when we'd arrived. He threw himself back in fright, slamming into the wall.

"Very impressive," one of the Warriors who'd emerged with the High Defender drawled. "You've successfully terrified a palace guard. I doubt that will work on the Sovereign."

"It might," Jay responded cockily.

There was an enormous foyer through the front door, the walls painted with a mural depicting dragons soaring through different landscapes, smiting enemies. The dragons looked nothing like Vall had, their bodies clumsy and their wings feathered like birds, and I wondered if the artist who painted it had ever actually seen one. How long had Vall said it was since the Warriors had been able to transform? Hundreds of years?

169

The High Defender took us past two more guards and down a wide corridor. More images had been painted on the walls. More dragons, just as wrongly drawn. They were going to have to completely redecorate at this rate, I thought. We approached a set of double doors, firmly closed with two guards standing in front of it. They nodded at the High Defender but didn't get out of the way.

"I need to see the Sovereign," he said.

One of the guards swallowed audibly, obviously uneasy, but he held his ground. "Forgive me, High Defender, but we've been given orders that the Sovereign is not to be disturbed."

There was a pause then the High Defender said, very carefully, "You are denying me entry?"

The guard shook his head immediately, then nodded. He looked wretched. "No, High Defender. That is to say, yes. The Sovereign said no one, sir."

Someone snickered, probably Jay.

"If I were you, I'd move," Vall commented idly.

The guard looked as if that was exactly what he wanted to do, but to his credit, he stayed put.

"I'm sorry, sir," he said. "I was told no exceptions."

The High Defender stepped forward until he was toe to toe with the guard. He was the same height, though his body was older, softer. I doubted he could take the younger man, but he had a presence that had both door guards quaking in their boots.

"Look at that female," he said quietly. Both guards fixed their gazes on me. "Count her markings. How many are there?" He waited, but neither guard answered. "What's the matter, can't count that high? How many fucking stars?"

"Seven, sir."

"That's right, seven stars. And if you were to go outside right now, you'd see another pair of idiot guards scratching their heads over shattered marble steps because a big bloody dragon just landed there. That dragon." He gestured to Vall, who grinned, showing all his teeth. "Get out of my way."

That was enough for the guard. He moved aside as fast as he was able, his compatriot fumbling at the doorknobs. He pulled them wide then got out of the way just quickly enough to avoid being run over.

As we followed the High Defender into the room, the pack shifted around me. Vall strode in front, with Finn and Jay on either side, Lyne protecting my back. It was comforting, having them surround me, but it also meant I couldn't see much around Vall's broad shoulders. I heard the Sovereign before I saw him.

There was a squawk, a squeal and an annoyed voice bellowed, "What is the meaning of this? I said I didn't want to be disturbed!" Something rustled and then the same voice shouted, "I'll have you executed! Useless idiots."

"They moved on my command," the High Defender said calmly. "It's me you'll need to execute."

"Oh. I see." The voice, which I assumed belonged to the Sovereign, sniffed. "Well, what is it? What do you want?"

We'd stopped in a large room, much more lavishly furnished. Curtains draped the windows and walls, four chandeliers hanging down from the heavily embellished ceiling providing light. I couldn't see the Sovereign, but I could see an enormous four poster bed, big enough to sleep ten people or, apparently, one king.

Stepping slightly to the side, pressing up against Finn, who didn't move over to give me more room, I finally got a glimpse of the Sovereign. He was unimpressive. The same copper-colored skin than Rin had had, he was lean and tall, his face all sharp angles. He wore lots of jewelry, rings through his ears and nose, necklaces around his neck, a gold chain dangling with charms tied around his stomach, held up by a ring through his bellybutton.

The jewelry was all he wore. Scowling heavily, he wrapped himself in a robe as a similarly naked pair of females scurried out of the room via a side door. The Sovereign watched them go with regret before turning back to the High Defender.

"Well?"

I saw the High Defender take a deep breath, to visibly calm himself. "Your Highness," he said. "You remember the Warrior, Vall Ridian?"

"Of course I know who he is," the king snapped. He stalked over, the robe only loosely tied. The High Defender was right, he'd definitely be jealous if he got an eyeful of Vall. "What is it? Have you come to tell me you've slaughtered those wretched sabers that desecrated the summer house? Good! You didn't need to interrupt me in my private time to tell me that!"

"They're not dead," Vall replied calmly. "I found them, but I didn't kill them."

The Sovereign's eyes bulged in his head. "I beg your pardon? I wanted them *dead*, how difficult is that? I—"

"Your Highness," the High Defender interrupted loudly. "That isn't why we're here."

"What is it, then? And why are those two Thinkers here? Didn't I ban them from the palace? Who else is there? Who's hiding? A female? Bring her forward!"

The pack tightened around me, hiding me further instead of obeying the Sovereign's command, and I lost my view of his outraged face.

"The female is part of it, sire," the High Defender admitted. "She's a seven-star female. Vall's pack has taken her to mate and she's enabled them to call forth their dragon." He paused. "They can fully shift."

Quiet descended for the space of a heartbeat, then I heard the Sovereign screaming, "Guards!"

CHAPTER TWENTY-ONE

Things had gone to shit incredibly quickly. As soon as the Sovereign started screaming for Warriors, Vall knew they were in trouble. They converged from all sides, spilling in through the double doors at the back, the side doors the Sovereign's females had run screaming through and a secret passage hidden behind the swathes of curtains draping the walls. At least twenty of them crammed into the room, claws unsheathed, teeth bared, ready to fight.

The threat to Lana had the dragon going crazy in Vall's chest. It wanted to come out. Even though he'd transformed only recently, Vall knew he could do it. If he did, though, there would be bloodshed. Every Warrior who stood against him would die, and he'd have to kill the Sovereign too, or he'd find himself facing the whole Triniun army. Breathing hard against the violence surging inside him, he gestured to his pack to stay put. He could feel their tension too.

"Hold!" the High Defender yelled.

"Arrest them!" the Sovereign contradicted.

The room descended into chaos as the Warriors closed in, then hesitated. The Sovereign was their leader, but he was a fucking idiot who couldn't tie his own shoelaces without two Thinkers to talk him through it, and the Warriors knew it. The High Defender was their commander, and his was the voice they were used to obeying.

"Hold!" he repeated. He waited a beat to be sure they were going to listen, then turned to the Sovereign. "Sire, calm yourself."

"I am calm!" the Sovereign screeched. He certainly looked it, with his ears pinned back, his eyes wide and rolling and his clawed hands clutching at the lapels of his fancy robe. He turned to the Warriors closest to him. "I want that pack arrested! What are you waiting for?"

The Warriors started forward, then froze as Ginn slashed his hand through the air, negating the order.

"You!" the Sovereign gasped. "You're in on it with them! You want my throne, don't you?" He gave a little scream, his expression manic. "You can't have it!"

"For fuck's sake, your highness, pull yourself together!"

Though the High Defender might denigrate the Sovereign behind his back, he'd obviously never spoken like that to his face. Vall watched his mouth open and close in astonishment. Ginn took advantage of his shocked silence.

"Vall is your loyal servant, your highness. He is not here to steal your kingdom from you, he's—"

But the Sovereign had stopped listening. He looked crazed, spit flying from his mouth as he pointed to some guards behind the pack.

"You! Get her! I want that female! Bring her to me!"

The guards—the same ones who had tried to stand against the High Defender at the Sovereign's bedroom door—had obviously learned their lesson. They didn't move.

If the Sovereign had been enraged before, now he was apoplectic.

"Did you not hear me? I said get her!" He paused for the space of a heartbeat, and when the guards still didn't move, Vall saw something snap behind his eyes. "Fine! Fine! I'll get her myself, I'll—"

He stormed forward, all but incoherent in his madness and reached out to lay hands on Lana, shielded in the middle of the pack.

Vall wasn't aware of making the decision to shift. One

moment he was a Warrior, disgusted at his king, the next he was the dragon with only one thought in his mind — protect.

There were screams and shouts as his body grew, bodies and furniture scattering to make way for him. Only his mate, his pack and the High Defender stood their ground. The Warriors were torn between awe and fear, many of them dropping to their knees, acknowledging his ascension to Alpha of them all. Vall hardly noticed, his attention fixed on the Sovereign, who had frozen on the spot, grasping hand still outstretched for Vall's mate.

Filled with a heady mix of outrage and protective rage, he snapped his teeth at that arm, intending to bite it off. He pulled up short when his mate — his *mate* — stepped in front of the Sovereign, her arms stretched wide.

"Wait!" she shouted.

Finn got himself in between Lana and the Sovereign a moment later, barging into the king and knocking him off balance. That broke his paralysis and he fled to the grand monstrosity of a bed like the coward he was.

Vall snarled, eyes flashing, making sure the male stayed there, then he looked down at his mate. The growl he had for her was lower, more intimate. She'd risked herself with that ridiculous move, and when he stood as a male again, he was going to make sure she knew it.

"Vall," she said, reaching out and patting his snout. "Be calm. You don't want to hurt him."

Vall snorted. Yes, he did.

She quirked a small smile, lowered her voice. "If you kill him you might have to be him, remember?"

That gave him pause, though he didn't like it. He could smell the stink of the Sovereign's fear and it made him want to chase, to hunt.

"Come back to me," she said softly. "Come back to me and let's talk this out."

Vall hated the High Council Room. It was baking in the summer, freezing in the winter and every time he'd ever been in here, he'd been fucked over in some way or another. He also hated the setup, the Sovereign raised up on his ridiculous throne, the eight highest members of the council—of which thankfully High Defender Ginn was one—perched slightly lower. Beneath them there was a wide-open space where whichever poor bastard had been summoned had to stand, getting a crick in their neck as they looked up at their exulted leaders.

He stood with Lana at his side, her fingers cold despite the suffocating heat and clutching at his, telling him how nervous she was. On his other side, Finn stood still as stone. Lyne and Jay had taken up defensive positions just behind, and then, behind them, every single Warrior in the palace had jammed themselves into the tight public galleries. When the five of them had been led into the room, escorted by Tan, Malin and Heo, Lana had been terrified, thinking the Warriors were there to contain them if things got out of hand.

They weren't, though. They were there to see the dragon. Vall didn't want it, but he felt it. He owned them all now.

High Defender Ginn was a Warrior, even if he was past his prime. He knew it too, knew that Vall had ascended to Alpha Warrior. The question was whether he'd shared that knowledge with the Sovereign or the wider council. None of them were Warriors, an unusual occurrence. The Sovereign had spouted some shit about how he wanted the highest minds to help lead the country, Thinkers and Administrators, but the truth was he was afraid of strength.

In which case, he was probably very, very afraid of Vall right now. And frightened people tended to do stupid things.

"With your permission, your highness, I'd like to call this meeting to order," began Councilor Jank, an Administrator who'd served so long that it was rumored he knew every law and legislation so well because he'd been there at the beginning when they were written. "We're here to discuss the situation of the blood thrall Lana—" He paused, peering at his notes.

"Ridian," Vall said, breaking protocol within the first sixty seconds. "Lana Ridian, Mate of Vall Ridian and his pack."

"Lana Ridian," the Administrator went on, his wrinkled face showing no hint of whether he was amused or annoyed at Vall's interruption. "And the claim that she is a seven-star female—" There were mutterings and gasps at this, several councilors leaning down to peer into Lana's face. "And that her blood is sufficiently pure to call forth the dragon in our Warriors."

"I would hardly call it a claim, Jank," Ginn cut in sarcastically. "Half the Warriors here witnessed him transform an hour ago."

"Still," Councilor Jank replied stiffly. "I would hear the evidence. I believe there are two Thinkers who have come to give testimony."

"Danin and Bern," Ginn confirmed.

Several on the council brightened visibly, and Vall remembered that the two Thinkers had been regulars at the palace, advising the Sovereign, before they retreated to their desert fortress.

"Bring them in, then," Councilor Jank instructed.

Danin and Bern were duly brought into the chamber. Bern seemed mildly amused by the whole thing, but Vall could see that Danin was sulking. Whatever falling out had happened between the pair and the Sovereign, Vall was betting Danin was at the center of it.

"You tested the female's blood?" Councilor Keron, a Thinker, asked.

"I did," Danin agreed. "I tested it and I gave her the

markings myself."

"She wasn't already marked?" Keron asked, confused.

"She hadn't been tested," Danin replied.

"All our females are tested at birth. How was she missed?"

Danin opened his mouth and closed it again, looking to Vall. It was Lana who answered. Though she was uncomfortable, her shoulders hunched with tension, she took a step forward and addressed the Thinker.

"Because I'm not from here. I'm not from this planet. I was in an accident on my world, and I think I died."

"You think you died?" Heavy skepticism lifted Keron's brow.

Lana shrugged. "I crashed my vehicle and everything went black. When I opened my eyes, I was here. I'd come through some sort of transporter and Rin—"

"An Administrator at the challenges," Vall interrupted.

Lana smiled at him, then faced Keron once more. "He said they couldn't be a female short in the challenges, and as I was here, he stuck me in. No one wanted me."

There was a loud snort at this, chuckles breaking out amongst the Warriors in the gallery.

"When Vall came in too late to compete, well . . ." She shrugged. "He was landed with me."

"I am sure he is not disappointed," Ginn commented.

"He just put her in, a stranger from who knows where? She could have had poison for blood for all he knew. She could have had some disease, infected us all!"

Vall didn't know much about the Administrator who spoke up now, his nose pinched in outrage, a sneer on his lips. He didn't like him, though. He especially didn't like the way he was looking down at Lana as if she was inferior, like she was some saber female who'd crawled in and crapped on the antique flooring. He growled, the sound low and rumbling and coming from his beast. The Thinker stared around in alarm, as if he was expecting a dragon to appear, before realizing it was Vall. He slunk low in his seat, his ears sliding back.

"Look, what are we doing here?" Councilor Balin finally barked. He was a Thinker who specialized in food cultivation, if Vall remembered rightly. He had a slightly grubby look about him, as if he'd been pulled away in the middle of a project—a project he was clearly thinking about getting back to. "So the Warrior can turn into a dragon. Terrific. The female's clearly not doing him any harm. If there was an issue with her blood, Danin and Bern would have found it. We all know they're the best. I don't see the problem."

"The problem," the Sovereign drawled, speaking for the first time, "is that this Warrior and his pack are a danger to the crown."

In the hour that had passed since the scene in the king's bedroom, he'd found some clothes, and apparently, his balls. He lounged in his gilded throne like a confident, competent leader, and the Thinkers and Administrators on the council, who didn't have a Warrior's sense of smell, couldn't scent the reek of his fear.

"A danger how?" Jay scoffed. He subsided when Vall turned to glower at him over his shoulder.

"This Warrior attempted to murder me in my bedroom," the Sovereign declared. "He transformed into a dragon and attacked me!"

"And yet you're not dead," Ginn pointed out mildly.

"Pure chance!"

"You threatened his mate."

"I am his Sovereign!"

"You are," Ginn agreed. "But mates are sacrosanct. Our very laws are built to protect them. And, as I said, he did you no harm. It was merely a warning."

"And the pack of Warriors he killed? The six he

slaughtered in their own den. What was that? I read the reports, they found them in *pieces*! He cannot be controlled, he —"

"That wasn't Vall," Finn interrupted. "That was me."

"You see!" the Sovereign exclaimed, jumping on Finn's words. "It's her blood, it's turning them into madmen!"

"You have transformed also?" Keron asked Finn, leaning forward in his chair. "You've become the dragon?"

"Not yet," Finn admitted.

"And yet you killed six Warriors?"

"They kidnapped Lana, threatened her. She fed me some of her blood and it gave me the strength to defend her."

"They kidnapped your mate?" Councilor Jank frowned.

"The Administrator Rin," Vall said. "We believe he must have given the pack details of Lana. There is no other way they could have known. And —" He grimaced. "We can't ask them now."

"Rin works for me," Jank said, clearly displeased. "I will find out the truth of this."

"I would appreciate that," Vall replied. Then his voice deepened. "If he is guilty, I would beg your leave to exact justice."

"If he is guilty, you'll have it," Jank promised.

"Let's get to the point of this, shall we," Keron interjected. "Do we or do we not believe that Vall and his pack are a threat to the crown?"

"You know, technically," Councilor Kilo, another Thinker, spoke slowly, ponderingly. "Warrior Vall would have the right to challenge for the Sovereignty. As a dragon, I mean."

He flicked his glance up toward the Sovereign as he said it, a smirk twisting at his lips.

"I don't want it," Vall said quickly. He wanted no part in ruling and he wanted no part in politics or whatever game Kilo was playing. "I want nothing more than my pack and my mate. I am happy to continue to serve as Warrior under High Defender Ginn." He gave the older man a short bow.

"But does your mate want you?" Councilor Jank asked quietly. "We've heard that you took her as your blood thrall, that you wish to claim her as your mate, but nothing from her. Does she accept?" He quirked his head, gestured toward the packed rows of Warriors. "She could have her choice of males. I daresay she could hold her own challenges." He looked down at Lana, his thoughts hidden behind his eyes. "Lana Ridian, I would have you speak. Do you take Vall and his pack as your mates?"

Lana turned to look at him, her face pale, her eyes unfathomable, and for a second Vall's heart froze in his chest. She was going to deny him, he thought suddenly. She was going to tear out his heart and hand it to the council. Then she smiled and the air returned to the room.

"I do," she said. "I am theirs as they are mine." She glanced back toward the rows of males who would walk on shards of glass to be given the chance just to speak with her. "I want no others."

Councilor Jank sighed. "Then really, Sovereign, I don't see what else there is to say. Warrior Vall and his pack want to be hers, she wants to be theirs, he still wants to serve the kingdom. Honestly, I think we should just let them go home and start mating, see if they can make some more seven-star females."

There was a titter of amusement at this, but Vall barely noticed. He was thinking about Lana, swelled with his babes. Was it possible? Danin and Bern would be able to find out and if it wasn't, he had faith the two Thinkers would be able to find a way to fix it.

High Defender took a deep breath and glanced around the council. "I believe Warrior Vall and his pack do not represent a threat to the kingdom. They and their mate have brought the dragon home to Trinia — I think they are its hope."

"Agreed," said Councilor Balin.

"Agreed." The same from Kilo and Jank. One by one the councilors gave a nod. The only person left was the Sovereign.

He took his time responding, his jaw shifting as he considered his words, gaze flicking back and forth between the council and the rows upon rows of Warriors, witnessing the proceedings.

"I have appointed a wise and noble council," he said at last. "I stand by their decision and I am . . .delighted that such majesty as the dragon has returned to our people."

The look he threw at Vall was full of utter loathing, but beneath the Sovereign, his face deliberately tuned away from his king, Ginn caught Vall's eye and winked.

CHAPTER TWENTY-TWO

Things were tense in the hover vehicle as we returned to the den. I didn't quite understand why—the meeting with the Sovereign had gone as well as we could have expected—but there was a heavy silence that I didn't know how to break.

Once we were safe inside the walls of the den, I realized I'd read the mood very wrongly. I'd barely cleared the door before Vall grabbed me, snatching me up in his arms.

"The bedroom," he said, his voice guttural. "Now."

I was tired, thirsty and hungry and I'd been thinking about the huge tub in the bathroom, feeling gritty and hot after the long drive back in the hover vehicle, but I immediately forgot all of these small discomforts when I saw the look in Vall's eyes, felt the possessive fire that he'd been keeping bottled up until we were home.

He swept me along, Finn, Jay and Lyne stalking us as we went, and I realized they were feeling it, too. Something had set them off and though I didn't know what it was, I was perfectly happy with the turn of events.

Though, when Vall dropped me down onto the bed and stood over me, arms folded, eyes intense and Finn, Jay and Lyne lined up on either side of him, vibrating the same primal carnality, it dawned on me just what I was in for.

I was apprehensive, but I was also panting with excitement.

"You claimed us as your mate in front of the council and the Sovereign," Vall said, voice low and heavy with emotion. "Did you mean it?"

"I . . .yes?"

He smiled tightly and shook his head. "No, little one. You have to be certain." He pierced me with his gaze. "Did you mean it?"

Did I? I hadn't wanted any of this. I hadn't wanted to die in a car accident because some asshole couldn't wait sixty seconds for a light to change. I hadn't wanted to be picked from a line up, handed over to a band of males for them to suck on my pulse points at will. I hadn't wanted to stay here, in this strange world, where my blood made me literal heroin to be craved.

I hadn't wanted any of that.

But it happened. I died, I woke up here and Vall got landed with me, the reject of the bunch. There was no going back. But that didn't mean I wanted to be their mate.

Their kindness did. Their protectiveness and their gentleness. The way they wanted to please me, the way they joked, the friendship that bound them together. The way they touched me, bringing me pleasure I'd never even dreamed of. All of it. That was why I wanted to be their mate.

"Yes," I said, my voice firm, my eyes solemn.

Four pairs of dragons' eyes stared back at me.

"Consider yourself claimed, Lana. Mate," Vall growled.

"Tell me we get to take her clothes off now," Jay said wickedly.

"We get to take her clothes off now."

The bed was large, but with four males piled onto it with me, it was still a tight fit. I felt them touching me everywhere, hands stroking and caressing, tickling my sides as first my tunic and then the trousers I was wearing were slid from my body. In between undressing me, they stripped as well, so that we were just one big, intertwined pile of bodies.

Vall took the lead, tucking me under him, sliding my legs apart so they wrapped around his hips. He leaned down and nuzzled at me before drawing back, our faces just inches apart.

"We're going to bring you such pleasure, beautiful mate, that you're never going to want to leave this bed."

"All of you?" I asked nervously.

"All of us," he repeated. "You can take it. In fact, you'll be begging for it."

My pussy clenched at the growl in his voice and I tilted my hips, already ready for him, but he pulled back.

As soon as he made a space, Jay and Finn filled it, Jay nipping and licking at my breasts while Finn slipped between my thighs, his tongue questing. The two were too much combined and I tried to close my legs, dislodge Finn, but Lyne took hold of one of my knees, keeping me spread wide. He smiled sexily as he did it, the fingers of his free hand running up and down the inside of my thigh.

"Too much," I said, not able to lie still while jolts of pleasure were rocking me from all over my body.

"No, it isn't." Vall's voice was full of dominance and I turned toward him instinctively, my dragon recognizing the calm in the storm.

"Can't," I told him, reaching out with a hand, needing him to anchor me.

"You can." He took my hand and tucked it against his chest, stroked my hair with the other. "Just relax. Feel. Let them touch you."

I closed my eyes, focusing on stilling my body. Jay was suckling me, the draws deep and causing the muscles in my lower stomach to clench. His fingers had trapped the nipple on my other breast and were rolling it, grabbing my attention with tight, sharp pinches that were little sparks of pleasure-pain. Lyne's touch was featherlight, but it was setting my nerves on fire, the trail of his fingers from my knee down toward the crease of my thigh drawing attention to Finn, who held my very soul in his hands as he circled and flicked, circled and flicked.

I wanted to draw away from it, to tighten up and fight the ecstasy they were wringing from me, but I forced myself to relax, to breathe, to let the pressure build until my orgasm slid over me in a rush that started gently but grew and grew until it stole my breath, stole my reason. I tried to cry out but I was paralyzed with pleasure.

When I came to, I had a death grip on Jay's hair, my thighs pressed tightly against Finn's head.

"Oh God," I gasped, unclenching my fingers and prying my legs apart. "I'm sorry, I'm—"

"Don't apologize for that," Finn said, lifting his head and gazing at me, smiling lips shiny with my release. "Or you'll be saying sorry for the rest of your life."

I hiccupped a small laugh, then squeaked as Vall shouldered Jay out of the way and lifted me up, arranging my limbs until I was straddling his lap, my arms wrapped around his neck.

"Ride me," he murmured. "Show me how you love your mate."

Conscious that I hadn't done anything except lie back and let Finn, Jay and Lyne bring me to a rip-roaring climax, I reached down to wrap my fingers around Vall's cock. He already had it in hand, though, was ready to guide it inside me.

"I want to touch you," I complained.

"Not this time," he told me. "We're claiming our mate, we pleasure you."

Weirdly turned on by his talk of mates and claiming, I shifted until I felt the head of his cock nudge my core, then slid down on him. From the way his eyes fluttered closed as I took all of him inside my body, the pleasure wasn't going to be all one-sided.

I rolled my hips, teasing both of us, and Vall's eyes

snapped open, the dragon in ascendance. His grabbed my hips, nails pricking the skin with exquisite gentleness.

"I said ride me." He punctuated the words with a short, sharp swat against my backside, just enough to sting.

Playing with fire, I ground down on him one more time. He tutted at me, but his grin was wickedly amused. I was expecting the crack of his hand on my rump this time, anticipating the heat that bloomed, then he put his whole hand over the area, a warning.

Finished teasing both of us, I rose up slowly and then slid down, my head tilting back as I felt every inch stretching me, stimulating sensitive nerve endings.

"Faster," Vall demanded.

I obeyed, moving into a rhythm that had both of us moaning, my hands clawing at his shoulders, his grip firm on my rear.

A hand stroked through my hair, swept it over my shoulder to bare my neck.

"Beautiful," Jay murmured in my ear. "I can't wait to feel you around my cock like that. I hope you make those little noises."

He started kissing along my neck, his hands running up and down my side, matching the tempo as I fucked Vall. I angled my head to give him better access, then whimpered as he pulled his hands away.

A moment later, Vall's hands shifted to my hips and I felt Jay's fingers trail over my left buttock. They kept going until they reached the center crease, then slid down, *down* until he found my rosebud with one finger. He circled it slowly, the feeling tickly but also strangely exciting, so that I was disappointed when he suddenly took it away. It was only for a moment, though, his finger returning slick with his saliva. He used that as lubricant to press down, break through the tight ring of muscle.

I gasped, uncertain and Vall's hands tightened on my hips. "It's all right," he said. "Just relax."

I did as he said, sliding deep and grinding down on him, Jay's finger moving deeper, stretching me wider.

"My finger today, my cock tomorrow," he murmured in my ear.

There was no way, not when I knew firsthand just how well-endowed Jay was, but the feeling of his finger, circling teasingly then sliding in and out, taking me to the first knuckle, then a little deeper, was a lot more erotic than I'd ever imagined. Just the idea of what he was doing was enough to hurtle me forward into my orgasm, my rhythm stuttering as pleasure swept over me.

Vall tightened his grip on my hips, done with being passive, lifting me up and pulling me back down, spiking my orgasm with each jolt.

"Oh God," I gasped. "Yes, more!"

"Are you talking to him or me, Lana?" Jay asked, his finger buried deep, stretching me, testing my limits.

"Both of you!"

He chuckled, kissing the back of my neck as Vall held me still and started thrusting upward in short, sharp jabs, chasing my orgasm with his own. I leaned forward, intending to kiss him, but his pulsing movements were nudging my g-spot just right, and all I could do was pant.

Finally he groaned, pressing up into me and mashing his face harder into mine, pushing his tongue into my mouth. We dueled gently as his body shuddered.

When he pulled back, it was to look at me with sated eyes. I smiled at him, my muscles jelly, but my pussy on fire, not quite satisfied. There were three other Warriors gathered round me on the bed, waiting, like predators on the hunt.

"More," I whispered raggedly. "I want more."

There was no mistaking the approval in his eyes. "Then

you'll have it."

Lifting me off him, Vall turned me around and leaned me back against his chest. He took both of my hands and tucked them down by his sides, keeping them there with a gentle grip around my wrists.

"Finn," he said. That was it, nothing else.

What more really needed to be said, though? Finn crawled between my legs, arms going under my knees and lifting them high. I was utterly helpless, trapped between the two males and I held my breath, seeing the fire in Finn's eyes and expecting the fucking of all fuckings.

He surprised me, then, when he paused, erect cock resting motionless against my pussy, the head pressing lightly on my clit and bent his head to kiss me. It was a sweet kiss, gentle.

He lifted his head so that he could stare down into my eyes. "Mate," he said.

Then he slid home, gentle and slow and long and thick. With my legs angled high, he went deep inside me, and I couldn't even cant my hips to relieve the pressure. I could do nothing but take it. He rocked back and forth a few times, letting me get used to the angle, the depth, then intensity sharpened the features in his face and he started fucking me in earnest.

There was no finger in my back passage in this position and I missed it. I glanced over Jay who winked at me wickedly.

"Tomorrow," he mouthed.

Tomorrow. I liked that idea, my hard *no* melting into a soft *yes*. The tight ring of muscle in question pulsed its agreement, causing me to clench around Finn, who gave a ragged groan.

"Come," he said. "I want you to come with me."

There was no way, not when I'd already had two orgasms, but I wanted it, craved the feeling of fire running through my veins.

"Come here," I gasped. "Kiss me."

He bent low and I met him on the way up, my teeth snapping at his lower lip, biting down hard. Finn jerked, pulling back, but not before I'd licked at him, drawing the bead of blood that sprang free into my mouth.

"More," I said.

Understanding, Finn slashed the cut deeper with his own fang, then kissed me again, tongue sliding against mine, offering me more of his blood to swallow. It took just a few more thrusts for me to feel it, a rush all over my body. It burst outward from my chest, and when it reached my pussy, where Finn was fucking me double time, slamming into me with firm strokes, I exploded.

"Yes!" I screamed, letting it consume me.

Finn powered home twice more before throwing his head back, roaring as he came.

"They are challenging us, Lyne," Jay commented, his voice coming to me through a hazy blur of pleasure. "Now we have to make her scream."

I could barely move, was spent with pleasure, my body coated with sweat and my heart thundering in my chest, but I reached toward the sound of his voice and felt hands transferring me.

I lay on my side, Jay cuddling up behind me while Lyne drew me against his front. He took my leg and hiked it over his hip, opening me up for Jay, who wasted no time sliding in from behind. This wasn't a fucking. It was a slow, sensual rock, his hand slipping round to cup my breast, holding it in the heat of his hand and flicking at my nipple with his thumb. In front of me, Lyne pushed my damp hair behind my ear and took my face in both hands. Asking nothing more, he kissed me, gentle and sweet, his lips plucking at mine, his tongue flicking into my mouth. He kept doing that until Jay shuddered, coming with a little moan.

"She didn't scream," Lyne commented quietly.

"I'm not done yet," Jay told him.

Staying deep inside me, he reached around and delved into my pussy, fingers finding my clit and circling it. He rocked against me, pressing a little harder and I started to writhe. Between his cock and his finger, I felt like a butterfly, trapped on a pin.

"Are you ready?" Jay asked.

He wasn't talking to me. Lyne nodded sharply and Jay slipped free, Lyne's cock replacing it in one swift move. He was hard and thick, even bigger than Jay, and I cried out, surprised.

"Now we'll make her scream," Jay said, low in my ear. "Come on, Mate. One last time."

His hand was pressed tight in between Lyne's body and mine, the heel of his hand putting pressure on my pubic bone. As Lyne fucked me with fast, even strokes, Jay spilt his fingers and slid them either side of my clit, squeezing it between them.

"Please!" I gasped, because the feeling was intense. My clit was supersensitive, and between Lyne thrusting against my g-spot and Jay's hand pressing down on my pubis, my pussy was screaming. I squirmed to get closer and to escape, but I was tucked in tight between the two of them—there was nowhere to go.

"I want you to scream," Jay hissed in my ear, just as Lyne gave a deft twist with his hips, hit me in a new way that had me crying out.

"Again!" I begged.

He did, thrusting again and again until I was all but delirious, then Jay let go of my clit, the blood surging back in, and thrummed his fingers over the top.

I screamed. Ecstasy blasted through me, blinding me, only the crush of Jay and Lyne's bodies holding me together. I twitched and juddered in their hold, nearly sliding off Lyne's cock as he powered his way to orgasm.

Afterward, all I could do was lie there. Gentle hands stroked me, rearranged me in the center of the bed. Cool cloths wiped the sweat from my skin, the combined slickness of our release from between my thighs. I struggled to open my eyes, exhaustion pulling at me. A firm hand rested on my forehead and Vall's voice ordered, "Sleep."

"Sleep with me," I mumbled.

He chuckled, then I felt him lie down beside me and gather me against his chest. Another body warmed my back. Finn, I thought, though I couldn't manage to open my eyes to find out. The bed dipped twice more as Jay and Lyne joined us on the bed.

"We're all here," Vall murmured. "Sleep now."

Surrounded by my pack, sore and exhausted but utterly satisfied, claimed, I slept.

CHAPTER TWENTY-THREE

My whole body was pulsing. Blood from Vall, Finn, Jay and Lyne sang in my veins. Danin and Bern hadn't suggested that was necessary, but I understood. They all wanted to play a part in this, know that they had a hand in my transformation.

Into a dragon.

I still wasn't convinced this would work. After a few additional feedings, Jay and Lyne were now able to shift, but that was different. The dragon might not have been as strong in them as Vall, or even Finn, but they were still Warriors. Still Triniun. I was human.

Still, I stood in the garden, the pack around me and the Triniun sun blazing down on my head and I hoped.

I wanted to fly.

I wanted to let the dragon I could feel sentient in my chest out and let her stretch her wings.

Most of all, I didn't want to disappoint the Warriors who were looking at me like I was their everything.

"Just relax," Vall murmured beside me. "There's no rush."

"I am relaxed," I argued.

"No, you're not."

Okay, I wasn't. I was excited and I was terrified. What if I could do it? Shift into a dragon—a freaking dragon—and lift up into the sky.

What if I couldn't?

"If you can't do it today, we wait a while and then we try again," Vall said, reading my thoughts.

"Uhuh." I agreed. I was twitching, on edge. I just wanted to get it over with, find out one way or the other. The beast in my chest was even more impatient. I could feel her pushing at my skin. Perversely, that just made me clamp down on her harder. What if she came out, but tore me up in the process? Scenes from *Alien* started running through my head, the creature bursting out of Gilbert Kane's stomach.

I clamped my lips together, worried I might puke.

"Finn, Jay, Lyne, you change first," Vall instructed. "Give her dragon some encouragement."

"How are three big, scary boy dragons going to encourage her?" I asked, slightly hysterically.

"Because she'll want to join them," Vall murmured seductively. "They're hers, after all. Her males."

I felt a throb in my chest as the dragon gave a jolt of agreement, and I was so agitated it made me cry out, clutching at myself as if I could hold her in.

"It's all right," Vall said quietly. "Calm, Lana."

"I'm trying," I told him.

He took my hands and gently pulled them away from where I had them, curled up tight against my body.

"We don't have to do this today. If you're frightened—"

I shook my head emphatically. "I want to try. I want to get it over with."

"We don't have to do it, ever," he said.

We did though. Because I had to know.

"I'm okay," I said, breathing deep and trying to mean it. "I'm ready."

Vall watched me for another long, careful moment, then gave the nod to Finn, Jay and Lyne. They stepped back to ensure they had enough space, and then they transformed. Though I found it slightly gross to watch—their skin stretched and grew, swelling then retreating, their faces distorting horribly before settling into shape—I made myself keep looking.

"Does it hurt?" I'd asked Vall that question before, curious, but now that I was facing doing the same thing, I felt the need to double check his answer.

"It's like a rush of heat," he assured me. "A stretch of your muscles. It's . . .satisfying."

"But does it hurt?"

His mouth curled into a small smile. "No."

The training space was large, but with three dragons now filling it, it was beginning to feel a little claustrophobic. They were enormous, scales glittering in the sunlight. There was nothing bulking or clumsy about then, though. Their muscles were sleek and well-defined. Despite their size, they were graceful. They shook themselves, Finn stretching his neck up high and giving a short, pleased trumpet, then each shuffled forward to gently touch their snouts to me before retreating to the edge of the training area, giving me as much space as possible.

It was time.

"Look at me," Vall said, stepping directly in front of me, both hands still clasping mine. "I want you to reach down to your dragon, feel her."

I nodded. I didn't need to reach for her, she was there, pounding her tail, demanding to be let out.

"Take a deep breath and step back. Let her come to the fore. She knows what to do. The only thing holding her back is you."

"Okay."

I tried to steady my breathing, closing my eyes and concentrating on my body. I could feel the tight bands I'd wrapped around the dragon, knew they were keeping her trapped. But unlocking them was a terrifying prospect.

Don't hurt me, I thought.

The dragon was too impatient, too visceral, to soothe me.

It just rocked, furious at the chains, demanding release. *All right, then.*

Taking a deep breath, I did what Vall said. I stepped back, let go of my hold.

It was like releasing the reins on a stallion, letting it plunge forward. I felt the dragon coil and then spring, surging up and out. Heat blazed along my nerves, an almost orgasmic release exploding through my muscles. The primal consciousness of the dragon rushed up to meld with my mind, our thoughts a chaotic mix of woman and beast. I was her, she was me.

Our eyes opened and Vall was there, down, lower than he had been, his large body dwarfed somehow. He was grinning, proud and triumphant all at once.

"There you are," he crooned.

Join us. We felt a surge of frustration because we couldn't speak the words, but it didn't matter. A moment later Vall was with us, quicksilver eyes on the same level, snout butting against ours. He angled his head, gesturing toward the sky and we looked upward, nostrils twitching, smelling the freedom of it.

Without giving us time to think, Vall took off, lifting up, beating his wings hard, tail flicking back and forth as if calling to us. And we wanted to join in.

We crouched low, muscles tensing, then thrust up, flapping our wings. Wings! Surprise and amusement in one mind, but both emotions dissolved into sheer joy as the world fell away and sky opened up.

We were flying.

Below, Finn, Jay and Lyne roared approval before launching their bodies up to join us. We soared on the currents, Vall at our side, the rest of the pack winging around us.

EPILOGUE

The chime came at the most inopportune moment. Danin held the vial with Vall's new blood sample in one hand, the compound he wanted to try adding to it in the other. He hissed out an annoyed breath, looking to the small screen connected to the front door security camera over on the far wall of the laboratory.

"Bern!" he shouted. Then, mind to mind, *Bern!*

There was no answer from Bern. He knew why. His partner in all things had won the frantic game of Batan they'd played, the victory handing him the right to delve into the secrets in Lana, Vall's seven-star female's blood. A bomb could go off above Bern's head right now and he still wouldn't notice. Danin could dance naked by his desk and get no response. He wasn't jealous—had he won the hand of Batan, he'd be exactly the same.

Maybe whoever was at the door would just go away.

He turned back to his workstation, lifting the dropper holding the compound and preparing to add it to the rich red of Vall's blood. Just a drop, just enough to test whether his theory was correct and the dragon's shift was controlled by the levels of—

The chime went again.

"For the love of—!" He was a Thinker, a scientist and a philosopher, resorting to foul language was beneath him, but if he spoiled this sample and had to go pleading to the Dragon Warrior for a more blood, if he had to wait until Vall had time to fit him into his suddenly very busy schedule, he was going

197

to call whoever had dared to invade their sanctuary every bad name he could think of. Right before he killed them.

Putting the vial of blood back into the tube rack and carefully returning the drops of the very volatile compound back to their home in the reinforced bottle, he stormed over to the console and slammed his hand down on the reader.

"What?" he barked, before the face had already been revealed. He didn't care if it was the Sovereign himself, Danin did *not* like to be interrupted while he was working.

It was almost as bad as the Sovereign — it was the High Defender. Luckily, Ginn was well versed in how Thinkers reacted when disturbed at their work. He didn't take offence, in fact, he even smiled into the screen. He must want something badly.

"Danin," he said. "Let me in."

"I'm busy."

"Oh." A quirk of Ginn's brow. "Should I come back tomorrow?"

"Come back next year."

The grin widened, humor and a hint of something slightly more lethal in Ginn's eyes.

"Open the door or I'll level this place and you'll be processing thrall testing samples for the rest of your life."

Danin was confident in the security measures that he and Bern had installed, turning what looked at first glance like an unassuming desert home into a veritable fortress, but Ginn was a tenacious bastard and he didn't make idle threats.

Teeth grinding together hard enough to crack, he jabbed his hand on the button to release the forcefield and buzzed Ginn inside.

He didn't go up to meet the old man, as courtesy and self-preservation demanded. He was too mad. Instead, he returned to his work bench and stared at the blood sample, just sitting there, waiting for him to unlock its mysteries.

"You know, some people actually like visitors," Ginn commented as he let himself into Danin and Bern's inner sanctum.

"Some people are fools," he snapped, refusing to turn around. If that compound didn't work, then perhaps . . .

"And here I came with a present for you. I know you're interested in the sabers."

Danin whirled around, piercing Ginn with a suspicious look. Now it was the High Defender's turn to ignore him, his attention down on the tablet he had in his hands.

How did he get that in there? Bern had systems in place to prevent unauthorized tech from getting into the laboratory, releasing viruses or hacking his systems and the myriad of secrets hidden there. He'd want to know just how Ginn had managed to get around his fail-safes.

And Danin would ask, later.

"Sabers?" he enquired delicately.

Ginn was laughing at him. He kept it studiously off his face, but Danin had known him for half his lifespan.

"Mmhmm."

Fingertips holding onto the last of his temper, Danin made himself ask, "What about them?"

Done playing, Ginn set the tablet aside and crossed the room to run his gaze over Danin's latest experiments. It was a disinterested perusal, Ginn was not a Thinker.

"You read Vall's report?"

"Of course." He'd devoured it and spent sleepless nights pondering every word.

"They're evolving," Ginn stated bluntly. "They're creating new tools, working with weapons. Their understanding of language is much greater than we realized and their speech seems to be hampered only by the fact their bodies aren't adapting as quickly as their minds. And then . . ." He took a deep breath. "They're inter-breeding."

Danin nodded. All of this had been in Vall's report.

"The Sovereign doesn't want to see it," Ginn went on. "He's blind in his hatred of them, thinks we can keep on doing the same thing we've been doing for the last millennia, squashing them like bugs. I need a way to change his mind."

"Hasn't he read Vall's report?"

"He had it read to him," Ginn replied bitterly, lip curling in disgust, "while he did his morning swim. He spent most of the time with his head underwater, how much do you think went in?"

Danin made a face. It would have been much easier if Vall had just bitten the Sovereign's head off, taken the throne himself. He might not want it, but he'd be a far superior leader. Of course, saying that was treason, even if the High Defender privately agreed with him, and Danin would find his own head separated from his shoulders if he voiced the opinion.

"What I need," Ginn went on, "is for the information to come from a respected source—"

"I'm not going to the palace again," Danin interjected quickly. "I have too much to do here."

"I don't want you to go to the palace," Ginn soothed. "I want you to go and study the sabers. I want you to go out there and take notes, do experiments, gather evidence, do whatever it is you Thinkers do and get me enough proof that the sabers are not animals, that they're people. A developing society perhaps, but people all the same."

It was a chance of a lifetime, the opportunity to go out and study a group emerging into civilization. To answer the call that had been pulling at Danin for as long as he could remember . . .but he already had the greatest discovery in an age sitting on his desk right here.

"I can't," he said, regret a heavy stone in his chest. "I have too much work to do."

"It doesn't have to be right away," Ginn soothed. "You have a little time—though Vall and Lana are not going anywhere. The sabers, on the other hand . . ." He grimaced. "The Sovereign ordered the destruction of a nest close to the Feld Reservoir just this morning."

Thoughts shifting through his head at breakneck speed, Danin looked down at the little vial of blood waiting patiently on him. He'd done his preliminary experiments and given report of his findings. Bern, too, had completed his most pressing inquiries, including ascertaining that Lana *could* bear young with Vall and his pack, should they choose. There was still much more to do, but did it have to be right now?

Torn, Danin stared at the High Defender.

"What makes you think he'll listen to me?"

"He won't," Ginn replied smoothly. "When he's made up his mind like this, he won't listen to anyone. He will, however, listen to everyone."

"I don't understand." And it wasn't often Danin got to say that.

"We don't take your findings to the Sovereign, we take them to the public. If we can make them more sympathetic to the sabers' plight, if we can get them to see the sabers as, well, as children just learning to walk rather than pests who need to be exterminated, we can manipulate the Sovereign into changing his stance. He's on thin ice at the moment and he knows it. He wants to keep the populace onside."

Danin pulled a breath in through his teeth. "It is a dangerous game you play. The Sovereign could have us executed for this conversation alone."

Ginn grinned. "If I avoided doing something because it might get me executed, I'd just sit about the house all day."

"I'll have to ask Bern. I'm not saying we'll do it," he hastened to add when Ginn's face creased into a smile.

"Of course," the High Defender replied smoothly. He picked up his tablet and gave a brief nod of farewell before letting himself out.

Danin listened to the sound of his heavy footsteps making their weary way up the stairs, then turned to look at his experiment, already looking forlorn and forgotten about.

"Damn," he muttered. "Damn, damn, damn." Then, raising his voice to a yell, "Bern!"

YOU MAY ALSO ENJOY THE FOLLOWING FROM EXTASY BOOKS INC:

When a Wolf Howls
Fiona McGier

Excerpt

"Well, this sucks." Saoirse McColl scanned the multiple internet links for appropriate jobs she could apply for.

"Can't apply to some of them because I know people who work there, who might sabotage my application by talking about me. Can't apply to others because I already know what it would be like to work there, and setting myself up for another failure is stupid. And the rest don't need my special skills, so they won't pay what I'm worth. What to do?"

She sighed and glanced around the empty room, discouraged. She was staying with her long-time best friend, so none of the furniture was hers, and she still felt like an intruder, even when the two other residents weren't home.

"Guess I'll have to keep sending out resumes and pestering HR departments for interviews. I need some kind of income-producing thing, and soon, or I'll be tossed out of this dump and have to live on the street."

"Why are you calling our home a dump?" Her longtime friend and roommate walked through the door, tearing off his nurse's uniform top as he strolled through the room into the kitchen.

"Oh, hey Freddie. Because I don't have any money to contribute to the bills, so I feel like a loser. I guess I'm taking my bad attitude out on everything around me."

"If you stay, I'm not any worse off than I was before you moved in." Freddie poured some chardonnay he pulled out of the fridge into a glass, then entered the living room and sat on the couch.

"But if I move out, you and Jorge can let one of your other friends move in . . . hopefully, someone who can help you pay the bills."

"When you moved in, you were helping."

"Yeah, but then I got fired again. Insubordinate, they called me. Just because I was following correct lab procedures, which made the tests take longer. So they said they had to let me go. I refused to cut corners, and I absolutely refused to fake data to produce the results their clients wanted. Hell, if even science is going to lie for corporations, then there's no one left to trust anymore. Right?"

Freddie took another sip from his glass, then shrugged. "I guess. You know I don't know anything about what you do at work. Or why you care so much. But that's a part of your charm, I guess."

"Your friends didn't appear to be nearly as taken with my charm as you are." She sighed. "Last night, when you had some people over, they seemed kind of uneasy that you have a female living with you. Almost like I'm some kind of different species."

He smiled. "Some of my friends are uneasy with anyone who is straight listening in on our conversations. Nothing personal."

"No, but some did tease you a lot about turning straight because you're allowing a woman to share your place."

"Then I explained that we've been friends since grade school and that ended, right?"

"Well, kind of. At least they stopped being actively rude to me."

"I seem to remember you saying you had to go meet some friends, and you left after about an hour."

"I lied. There are acquaintances that I used to work with, but you're the only friend I have in this city. My family is mostly all back in Chicago. You know us Irish . . . we tend to stay where we landed when we got here. And Chicago is a city of neighborhoods, where even in the middle of urban crowds you can choose to live among people who look like you."

"Yeah, you can even find places where people think like you. I liked Chi-town's Boystown for a while. But when I got the offer to move out here to Boston, I realized that you can find like-minded folks everywhere. You just have to be open to finding them."

Freddie stared at her, serious for a moment before smiling. "Maybe that's your answer, Sam. You need to be open to new people and hope the universal karma will toss in folks who think like you, and who will appreciate you, your way."

"And just how am I supposed to do that? It's not like heading into the local gay bar to find other gay folks. There aren't any science bars where geeky researchers hang out. Where am I supposed to go to find people who believe in doing the best job they can, and who don't let money issues dictate what to research? People who want to help people improve their lives through science, but who still want to be able to afford to pay the bills?

"Even when I was working full-time, I barely had enough to pay a third of the rent on this place. I was just lucky that you and Jorge were all right with me crashing on the air mattress in your spare room when I was desperate for a place to stay. And that you took pity on an old friend and let me mooch off your good nature."

He got up and pulled her out of her chair for a big hug.

"Honey, you know I'd do anything for you. We go way

back. Remember when you beat up Danny O'Toole when that snot called me a faggot in fourth grade?"

She nodded, smiling. "Yeah, he didn't expect a girl to be able to hit so hard. I guess he didn't know that I had six brothers who made me fight them frequently, just to keep themselves in shape. I guess they did teach me how to protect myself."

He laughed. "And others. Danny ran away crying, with blood gushing from his nose. I don't think he underestimated girls after that."

"At least not me, anyway." She smiled and sat back down. "I didn't even know what a faggot was back then. I was just pissed that he was insulting my best friend."

Freddie resumed his position on the couch. "And honey, I sure was glad we were besties, especially since other guys thought twice about messing with me after that."

"Well, it was never fair that they would gang up on you, either because you were Black, or because you were gay. They needed to know that you had a crew who would fight with you. Even if your crew only consisted of one girl with a redhead's temper."

Saoirse was lost in thought for a few minutes, reminiscing.

Then Freddie broke the silence. "No luck with the job search today, then? Is that why you're in such a pissy mood?"

She sighed. "Yeah. There are only a few labs around doing the kind of research I'm interested in doing. Most of them I've either worked for or know people who work there, who would advise their bosses not to hire me. I don't know what to do anymore."

Freddie tapped his phone and began to scroll through things quickly. He stopped after a few minutes and looked back up. "Why don't you think about something completely different?"

"Like what?"

"Well, here's an ad for a high school biology teacher."

She snorted. "I can't even get along with adults. What

makes you think I could get along with teenagers?"

"You're very good with troubled people. I can't think of any time in my life when I was more troubled than in high school. You talked me out of a whole lot of stupid mistakes, and you picked me up and helped me recover after the bad ones I did make. Maybe that's your calling?"

"I don't have any teaching certification."

He scanned the ad again. "It says teaching experience preferred but not required. It's a private school, up in northwestern Maine. See?"

He passed his phone over, and Saoirse read the ad.

"Hmm, it says you would have to live on the premises, but living quarters are provided. It also says that the school lab needs to be updated and remodeled, so the new teacher would be expected to help with that project. I would really love the chance to design a lab myself. I have so many ideas about what to put into it, and what not to."

"And you have a master's degree in biology, right? You're a researcher. If anything, you're probably over-qualified. But as long as the salary is decent, them supplying you with a place to live would enable you to not have to pay rent anywhere."

"Yeah . . ."

"Honey, what can it hurt to apply?"

"How will I be able to afford to get up there to interview?"

"You have a birthday coming up, right? I can pay for you to fly up there and rent a car to get to the place."

She smirked. "Just so you can get rid of me?"

He tossed a pillow at her, which she just barely avoided by ducking in time for it to fly by her head.

"No, silly bitch. So I can repay you for all of the times you held my hand when I needed a friend."

Saoirse shrugged. "I grew up in a big family, remember? Lots of people around all the time, many of whom needed a listening ear followed by hugs . . . or a slap upside the head. It's not any special kind of skill."

"No, but damn few people know how to do it as well as you. So apply, already."

She picked up her laptop and typed in the e-dress that was listed in the ad. "Okay, it's worth a shot, I guess. I wonder what kind of area it's in. Northwestern Maine is pretty rugged, right? No big city pollution up there. Worst-case scenario is I don't hear anything back from them."

"A better case is you get to fly to a state you've never been to and rent a new-ish car to drive into the countryside. You like that better than city driving anyway, right?"

"Uh-huh." She was distracted by filling out the application form.

"Let me get you a glass of that sparkling wine you like . . . I think there's an open bottle in the fridge, right?"

"Uh-huh."

"Good luck, girlfriend."

ABOUT THE AUTHOR

Charli Mac is a Scottish writer and former English teacher now living in sunny Colorado. She writes erotic romance with a sci-fi/ fantasy twist, but is also an award-winning Young Adult novelist, which she writes under a pseudonym. Her YA novels have been translated into more than fifteen languages and sold in excess of four million copies. Her favorite things are hot alpha males and the nerdy, curvy women they love.

www.ingramcontent.com/pod-product-compliance
Lightning Source LLC
Chambersburg PA
CBHW070832120626
46556CB00002B/729